Grimgar of Fantasy and Ash

level. 3 — You Have to Accept That Things Won't Always Go Your Way

Presented by Ao Jyumonji Illustrated by Eiri Shirai

"We anticipate that the enemy boss, the keeper, will be in one of these three towers."

Bri-chan spread out a map on the ground, illuminating it with a lamp. It looked like a map of the main keep at Deadhead Watching Keep.

"Yeah! That's right!
You're no dull-witted oaf!
You're doing great, Moguzo!"

He was like a totally different person.
No. Maybe this was Moguzo.

"I'M NOT A DULL-WITTED OAF!"

Moguzo attacked, swinging The Chopper around left and right. He continued his assault without ever giving his enemy a moment to catch his breath.

The Story So Far

"Awaken."

On hearing that word, Haruhiro awakens to find himself in the unfamiliar world of Grimgar.

In order to survive, Haruhiro and the others are forced to live as volunteer soldiers. Despite losing Manato, the central figure of their party, Haruhiro and the others add a new priest, Merry, to their group. As they grow a little, they graduate from being trainees.

When Team Haruhiro decide to challenge themselves by going to the Cyrene Mines, they struggle there, but they also improve themselves little by little. While there they experience an incident where Ranta is separated from the party, and fight with Merry's former comrades who have risen as undead. Merry succeeds in exorcising her erstwhile companions.

While everyone is taking a rest, Death Spots attacks. The party is driven to the brink of destruction, but they are saved by a single blow struck by Haruhiro. The party rejoices, but somehow it just doesn't feel real to Haruhiro.

They have survived another day.

And so, the adventure continues.

Grimgar of Fantasy and Ash

level. 3 — You Have to Accept
That Things Won't Always Go Your Way

Presented by
AO JYUMONJI

Illustrated by
EIRI SHIRAI

GRIMGAR OF FANTASY AND ASH, LEVEL. 3

© 2014 Ao Jyumonji
Illustrations by Eiri Shirai

First published in Japan in 2014 by
OVERLAP Inc., Ltd., Tokyo.
English translation rights arranged with
OVERLAP Inc., Ltd., Tokyo.

Seven Seas books may be purchased in bulk for promotional,
educational, or business use. Please contact your local
bookseller or the Macmillan Corporate and Premium Sales
Department at 1-800-221-7945, extension 5442, or by
e-mail at MacmillanSpecialMarkets@macmillan.com.

Follow Seven Seas Entertainment online at gomanga.com.
Experience J-Novel Club books online at j-novel.club.

Translation: Sean McCann
J-Novel Editor: Emily Sorensen
Book Layout: Karis Page
Cover Design: Nicky Lim
Copy Editor: Tom Speelman
Proofreader: J.P. Sullivan
Light Novel Editor: Jenn Grunigen
Production Assistant: CK Russell
Production Manager: Lissa Pattillo
Editor-in-Chief: Adam Arnold
Publisher: Jason DeAngelis

ISBN: 978-1-626926-62-2
Printed in Canada
First Printing: October 2017
10 9 8 7 6 5 4 3 2 1

[TABLE OF CONTENTS]

Characters

YUME
Airheaded soothing-type. Speaks an iffy sort of Kansai dialect?
Class: Hunter

HARUHIRO
Sleepy eyes. Passive-type. Provisional leader.
Class: Thief

SHIHORU
Shy and withdrawn. Hard worker with little presence.
Class: Mage

RANTA
Selfish, flaky joker. #1 most unpopular.
Class: Dread Knight

MERRY
Cool beauty. Has more experience as a volunteer soldier and is a little more of an adult.
Class: Priest

MOGUZO
Bear-type. A somewhat slow, but reliable bear.
Class: Warrior

Team Renji

Ron – Class: Paladin – The Team's No. 2.
Sassa – Class: Thief – Flashy woman. Probably an M.
Adachi – Class: Mage – Wears glasses.
Chibi – Class: Priest – Mascot.

Day Breakers

Kemuri – Class: Paladin
Pingo – Class: Necromancer
Shima – Class: Sword Dancer
Lilia – Class: Shaman

Other

Kikkawa – Class: Warrior
Hayashi – Class: Warrior
Michiki – Class: Warrior
Mutsumi – Class: Mage
Ogu – Class: Thief

Grimgar of Fantasy and Ash

Other Characters

RENJI

Head of Team Renji.
Wild beast-type. Dangerous.

Class: Warrior

MANATO

Kept the party together.
Was a good guy. (Past tense)

Class: Priest

SOMA

Started the Day Breakers Clan.
Seems to have some objective.

Class: Samurai

Grimgar
of
Fantasy and Ash

1. Social Status, Talent, and a Slight Bitterness

"Ranta! Don't wander off too far!" Haruhiro cautioned.

Even as he said that, he got in position behind a kobold foreman Moguzo was exchanging blows with and started to look for an opening.

Yeah, there are openings, he thought. *Lots of them.*

There was one a moment ago. Right then, too. We can do this. We can.

The foreman was shaking its tail and moving around a lot, but Haruhiro had a grasp of its quirks. When Moguzo attacked a certain way, he knew how it would defend, and then he had a good idea what it might do after that. He could finish this with Backstab or Spider— of that he was confident.

And yet, Haruhiro didn't close in on the foreman. Because that wasn't the point.

Haruhiro was after something else.

Will I see it? he was wondering. *That line.*

That vague, hazy line that shone just a little.

If he could just see that.

"That line you saw is something anyone who's gained some

experience will have seen once or twice—or felt, rather. That might be the more correct way to describe it." That was what Barbara-sensei from the thieves' guild had said to him. "Sometimes I see it, sometimes I don't. It's not something you can see by focusing, after all."

"That's not a bad sign," she'd said, as well.

"However, don't misunderstand. It's nothing special," she'd made sure to point out.

It was a thing anyone who gained some experience would see once or twice. However, Haruhiro had seen that line a good number of times. Even the time he'd taken down Death Spots—no, that time the line had been clearer, more defined. If he hadn't been able to see that line, Haruhiro would never have been able to slay Death Spots. That giant kobold would have thrown Haruhiro off and chased down the rest of the party.

If that had happened, there could have been casualties. Someone might have died.

Haruhiro had—no, Haruhiro *and* the party had been saved by that line.

What if it'd been pure coincidence that he'd been able to see it? Just then, at the perfect time, he'd happened to see it by chance. What if that was all it was?

It'd mean fortune had been on his side then. Haruhiro had gotten lucky. Without that fluke, they might've all died.

I don't want to think I just got lucky—do I...?

Haruhiro honestly didn't know, but he knew for sure that being able to see that line would help him. He wanted to see it.

If possible, I want to have complete control over when I see it.

Whenever I want, however often I want, if I could see the line on those terms—Just maybe, I'd be kind of invincible...?

It's not that I want to be invincible, that's not it. But, if I can get stronger, if I can gain a power that'll give me that decisive edge in battle when I need it...

"Thanks...!" Moguzo shouted.

While Haruhiro was thinking about the line, the line, and nothing but the line, Moguzo used Thanks Slash, or what was more properly known as Rage Blow, to hit the foreman with the most powerful diagonal slash he could muster. Moguzo's blade buried itself fifteen to twenty centimeters deep inside the foreman's shoulder. The foreman's chain mail armor didn't do anything to stop it.

Moguzo's dumb, brute strength is a thing to behold, Haruhiro thought. *However, there's more to it than that. It's the sword.*

His cleaving blade, The Chopper.

After discussing it as a group, ultimately they'd gone with Ranta's suggestion, and that was what it'd been named.

It was only about 1.2 meters long, which wasn't that long, but it was fairly thick. While it did have a hand guard, it gave off the impression of a gigantic carving knife.

That thing came from Death Spots. I'm impressed he can wield it so well.

"Hungh...!" Moguzo kicked the foreman to the ground. Without missing a beat, he slammed The Chopper down on the foreman's head, smashing it open with a wet thud. "Next...!"

Somehow, I feel like I can rely on him.

While he was busy admiring Moguzo...

"Haru!" Merry shouted.

"Huh?! Wh-what...?!" he stammered.

"What do you mean, 'What...?!'" Ranta demanded.

I don't want to hear that from you, Ranta, but, well, I guess I kind of deserve it.

Haruhiro and the others had been frequenting the third level of the Cyrene Mines—a residential area for kobold workers—where their hunts mainly targeted elder kobold foremen. The talismans the foremen carried, while they could be hit or miss, sometimes sold for a high price, and now that Death Spots was gone, there wasn't much danger on the third level. It was a good hunting ground for making a constant income.

Even so, this was a stronghold of the kobolds, a hostile race, so it wasn't without danger. Actually, if they let their guards down, they would pay for it.

Moguzo had taken down the foreman, leaving only two followers. Ranta was taking on Follower A, while Yume and Merry were clobbering Follower B. With the scary foreman taken care of, it was easy to think this'd be an easy win, but it was the way of the world to betray such expectations.

Because here another foreman came, three little minions in tow, energetically running towards them.

"Six..." Haruhiro whispered, having done some quick mental math, but then Moguzo bellowed "Thanks...!" and slammed The Chopper into Follower B, the one Yume and Merry had been facing.

"...Ah. Five," Haruhiro said.

"Why, you...!" Ranta shouted.

Ranta and Follower A had locked blades—or so it seemed, but then Ranta knocked the follower back with a loud clang.

That was his newly learned dark fighting skill, Reject. When an enemy gets in close, he uses his sword to push them back and gain some distance. It's a rather plain skill. Considering Ranta's personality, I'm amazed he decided to learn it. Though, if he follows Reject up with another skill, it leads to good combos.

"Anger!" Ranta shouted.

Once Follower A was pushed out of range, Ranta stepped in, stabbing at its gullet.

I'm disappointed in myself. Just now, for a brief moment, Haruhiro had thought Ranta was cool.

Ranta hasn't just learned a new skill; because he's not able to use his beloved bucket helmet anymore, he went and bought a visored helmet called a bascinet. He bought it used and it was darkened with tarnish, but he was probably thinking something stupid like that that just made it a better fit for a dread knight like him. Though, as a matter of fact, it does make him look kind of dread knight-y, and maybe just a little cool.

"Wait, it's four now!" Haruhiro hastened to give orders. He was technically the leader, after all. "Moguzo, take the foreman! Ranta, one of the followers is yours! Take it out as quick as you can! For the other two, Yume and I'll manage them for now...!"

With a shout, Moguzo charged the foreman, crossing blades with it. He used Wind to make it back down, then pushed, pushed, and pushed some more.

"Hatred...!" Ranta leapt at Follower C. It dodged his first slash, but with one blow coming after the next, he was still pushing it back.

Follower D charged straight at Yume, but when it swung its shovel down at her, Yume let out a cat-like cry and did a low backwards somersault to avoid it.

That was Weasel Somersault, which she just learned. It's a machete fighting skill. I don't feel like it's directly related to fighting with a machete, though.

As Follower D was looking surprised, Yume closed in on it. She executed a combo with Brush Clearer and Diagonal Cross. Follower D was faltering.

"I can do something, too!" Haruhiro called.

Haruhiro didn't particularly want to show off, though, and taking on enemies in straight up fights wasn't a thief's specialty. Follower E came at him swinging its shovel. With not just the blade but the handle being made of metal, it was a sturdy shovel that could be used for both combat and digging holes. Haruhiro knocked it aside with his dagger.

Swat.

Swat.

Swat.

Swat was primarily a defensive skill, but when the opportunity arose, it could be used like this, too.

When Follower E went for a big swing with its shovel, Haruhiro dodged it, deliberately choosing not to use Swat this time. Follower E mustve sensed the danger, because it quickly pulled back its shovel, using more compact swings from then on. It was focusing on speed over power.

"Ngh...!"

Haruhiro used Swat. A strong hit, meant to push the shovel away from Follower E's body.

As a result, it created an opening.

Haruhiro got in close, seizing Follower E's right arm with his left hand and his own right arm. Follower E yelped as he bent its elbow to an extreme, then he swept the legs out from under it, knocking it over.

It was a fighting skill Barbara-sensei had taught him—or, rather, like she always did, beat into him—Arrest.

It feels good to pull it off, but it sure isn't showy.

Haruhiro stomped on the fallen Follower E's jaw, dislocating it. Kobolds had a dog-like head, giving them a lot of bite strength, but their jaws themselves weren't especially sturdy. They were especially weak against strikes that came from the side. Follower E passed out, or went into a state close to it.

"Ohm, rel, ect, palam, darsh!" A shadow elemental that looked like a mass of black seaweed launched from the tip of Shihoru's staff, flying forward in a spiral. "Yume!"

"Yikes!" Yume cried, crouching down as the shadow elemental soared over her head and collided with Follower D. The shadow elemental worked its way into Follower D's body through its nose and ears. As soon as it did, Follower D stood there, staring into space.

The confusing shadow, Shadow Complex.

Despite saying she wanted more attack power, the new Dark Magic spell Shihoru had learned was one that affected the target's brain and caused a state of confusion. It was similar to the one that lulled them into a deep state of sleep, Sleepy Shadow, but Shadow Complex would also work on enemies that were prepared for it or were in a state of heightened emotions. It was the sort of choice Haruhiro would expect from Shihoru, and it was useful in its own way.

Despite Yume being right in front of it, Follower D threw its shovel away and clutched its head.

"Meow, meow, meow, meow, meow!" Yume unleashed a flurry of

blows on Follower D. It seemed Follower D noticed, but it was much too late for it to do anything. By that point, it was slashed up so badly, there was no way it could have turned things around.

"Why, you...!" Ranta used Reject to push his opponent back and Anger to finish it, taking down Follower C with the combo he'd been using a lot lately.

"Ungh...!"

Is Moguzo struggling against the foreman? No. That's not it.

Just now, the foreman's sword had hit Moguzo's left arm, but he must've allowed it to. Moguzo had bought some reasonably priced arm and waist guards used and then paid an armorsmith to resize them for him. He'd also learned one heavy armor fighting skill.

The foreman's sword bounced off of the armor on Moguzo's left arm with a clang. It hadn't been deflected in the normal way, though.

Steel Guard.

Not being a warrior, Haruhiro didn't really understand it, but it was a skill that knocked away enemy attacks using defensive gear and particular methods of applying power.

Incidentally, Haruhiro and the others currently had their athletic ability, their resistances, and their natural healing boosted by Merry's new light magic spell, Protection. Maybe it had something to do with the symbol of the god of light Lumiaris being a hexagram, but its effect covered up to six people for a period of thirty minutes. When the spell was cast, a hexagram of light would appear on their left wrists, their bodies would feel noticeably lighter, and they'd be in top form.

Thanks in part to that, Moguzo was able to pull off his next move with panache.

Of course, he used that one: "Thanks...!"

It was the one that'd become a fixed feature of all their fights, with both power and stability, the Thanks Slash.

With the foreman's sword deflected and it knocked off its balance, Moguzo slammed The Chopper down on its shoulder. It was nearly identical to when he'd killed the first foreman.

Moguzo may not look it, but he's pretty skillful, and he doesn't try to act cool or come up with little tricks like Ranta. He's straightforward in a good way, you could say. He sticks to basics, and as he repeats the same actions, he perfects them in his own way—If I praise him that much, I may be overstating it, but Moguzo's Thanks Slash is definitely turning into a killer move.

Of course, there are his strength, his polished technique, and the quality of his weapon, among other things, that go into it, I'm sure, but, anyway, his timing is good. The Thanks Slash always shows up at the ideal moment. It makes me want to applaud. Maybe I will.

While Haruhiro was wondering whether to or not, Ranta came up behind Follower D, which Yume had been working on cornering, and brutally took it down.

"Yeah! Got my vice...! Mwahahahaha...!"

"Augh! What're you doin'? Yume coulda handled that one by herself!" she complained.

"What? You wanted to kill it yourself? Hah! You may have tiny tits, but you're a bloodthirsty wolf, you know that? Are you going to convert and start worshiping Lord Skullhell like me now? Hmm?"

"Nuh-uh, no way. Yume's a hunter. And Yume loves her white god Elhit-chan, too. Yume just thinks, since she was facin' that kobbie in solar combat, she shoulda kept it that way to the end! Also, don't call my boobs tiny!"

"Yume, you mean solo combat." Haruhiro tried to correct her because he couldn't bear not to, but, as per usual, he was completely ignored.

"It just goes to show, girls with tiny tits can't do anything! If you don't like that, make 'em bigger!" Ranta mocked.

"You say that, but Yume, she doesn't know how to make her breasts get bigger!"

"Huh?! You do this..." Ranta mimed squeezing his own chest.

Shihoru looked at Ranta with disdain, such incredible disdain. "...That's sexual harassment."

Merry sighed a little. "You're *terrible*."

"Damn straight!" Ranta said, standing tall. "I'm fine with being a harasser! And fine with being terrible! Keep it coming! Don't think you'll make me back down with just that! If that's what you're going to call me, I'm gonna become the terrible king of sexual harassers!"

"Murrgh," Yume mimed squeezing her own breasts—or, rather, actually squeezed them. "If Yume squeezes 'em, her breasts'll grow bigger? If that's all it takes, it's not so hard, huh?"

"Bwuh!" Moguzo spewed out whatever was in his mouth.

"Y-Yume..." Shihoru grabbed Yume by the arm, stopping her. "I-I don't think you should do that in front of other people..."

"Huh? Does it work better if Yume does it when no one's around?"

"No, uh... That's not the problem..."

Ranta laughed derisively. "Your pitifully tiny tits ain't big enough to squeeze anyway, so you don't need to worry about it. Gwahaha!"

"Augh! Ranta, you dummy!" Yume wailed.

"I'm no dummy! I'm the terrible king of sexual harassers! Freshly crowned! Revere me!"

"Don't get so stubborn..." Haruhiro muttered.

Haruhiro started checking over the kobold bodies. Their equipment and other stuff wouldn't sell for enough to be worth the extra weight, so he was fine with just collecting the talismans.

When he crouched down next to a follower and began to carefully remove an earring, Ranta came running over. He quickly tore a golden nose ring off a follower that was right next to the one Haruhiro was working on.

Come on, that crudeness is what people don't like about you, Ranta, Haruhiro thought. *Well, that and a whole lot of other things. Actually, they dislike pretty much everything about you.*

"Huh? What's your problem?" Ranta glared at Haruhiro. "You got something to complain about?"

"...Not really."

"Well, I do."

"Huh?"

"About you, Haruhiro," Ranta flipped the golden nose ring with his thumb, catching it in the palm of his hand. "Man, I think you're misunderstanding something."

"Misunderstanding? Huh...? What're you on about?"

"In other words, it's like this. I hope you don't want to be a hero or something like that, do you?"

"A hero?" Haruhiro asked.

Since it was coming from Ranta, he had to just be spouting nonsense. That was what Haruhiro thought at first. However, once he mulled over the words, he felt a weight quickly building in his stomach.

A hero.

I'm no hero.

I've never even thought I want to become one. I haven't—but...

I really don't want to be a hero, not in the least. It's just...

Just—What exactly?

"Earlier..." Ranta said, lowering his voice. He was trying not to be heard. Could he possibly have been trying to be considerate somehow? Even though this was Ranta? "...The way you were moving was weird, man."

"...No, it wasn't."

"No, seriously. It was strange. If I were to go further, I'd say you were the only one acting strange. It was like you were going at a slower pace, I could say. Maybe that's not it. That's not quite how I'd describe it. Or maybe it is. Well, either way, doesn't matter. I know what you were up to. You were trying to take them down with one blow, weren't you?"

Haruhiro just shrugged a little, giving no answer. He did his best not to show any change of expression, but he was sweating inside. Because Ranta was dead on.

This was *Ranta*. How had he figured it out?

"It's not like you, Haruhiro, you know that? Hmm? You ought to know your place. Okay?" Ranta slapped him on the shoulder.

Haruhiro had a strong urge to knock Ranta flat, but he refrained.

Even if I told you, there'd be no point. Would you understand? You, Ranta? I don't think so.

Ranta couldn't possibly understand how Haruhiro felt.

Haruhiro had nearly died. He'd meant to give his life so his comrades could escape.

True enough, his comrades had been fine, and Haruhiro hadn't had to die. On top of that, he'd even taken down Death Spots. It had gone great.

The result had been great, but he couldn't just say, "All's well that ends well."

After all, he'd just gotten lucky.

Had he not happened to see the line that time, Haruhiro couldn't have killed Death Spots.

But I did see it, so what was wrong with that? I shouldn't take it lightly like that.

If he got in a similar situation again, would he leave his fate to the heavens then, too?

He couldn't do that. Well, what could he do, then?

There were two things.

One was to avoid getting into a life or death situation again. Of course, he intended to be careful not to.

Then there was the other option: make it not a fluke. He just had to make it so he could see that line at all times.

But, it doesn't work like that. Even Barbara-sensei said, "Sometimes I see it, sometimes I don't. It's not something you can see by focusing, after all." It's unreliable. It's a mistake to try and count on it. I know that.

But maybe, Haruhiro might have been thinking, *it wasn't a fluke at all. I might have some sort of talent.*

...If I do, that'd be nice.

"Haru?"

"Huh?"

When he looked up, Merry was crouched down next to him.

"Wh-what? Huh? I-Is something up...?" he asked.

"I should ask you the same," Merry said, laughing a little. "Worried about something?"

"Nah—"

If this hadn't been the third level of the Cyrene Mines, and Merry had been the only one around, would he have opened up to her and been honest?

Even then, he might not have.

"It's nothing," he said.

"I see. Well, that's good, then."

The look on Merry's face told him she didn't think it was good at all. Haruhiro felt a dull pain in his chest, as if he'd done something wrong.

It's kind of unfair, you know. All of this stuff.

Grimgar
of
Fantasy and Ash

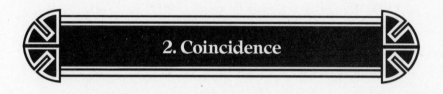

2. Coincidence

They returned to Alterna, sold off their loot, split the proceeds, ate dinner, returned to home sweet home at the volunteer soldier lodging house, bathed, went back to their rooms, and then all that was left was to go to sleep. That was all, yet Haruhiro couldn't get in the mood to do so.

The hanging lamp on the wall had already been put out.

That lamp, and two bunk beds stuffed with hay. That was all there was in this room.

I want to say farewell to this place and find a better room to stay in. It's an option now, but I just can't take that leap.

Haruhiro was lying down in his upper bunk. Moguzo was in the lower bunk of the bed next to him, while Ranta was on the top one. There were three of them in a four-person room. In the beginning, the room had been at capacity, and there'd been four of them.

Haruhiro was about to quietly call their lost comrade's name, but he stopped himself.

When he came down from his bunk...

"...Haruhiro-kun?" Moguzo called out to him. "Is something up?"

Ranta was snoring loudly. It seemed he was asleep.

"Uh... Yeah." Unable to come up with a good answer, Haruhiro was vague. "Well, it's not really that anything's up."

After saying it, he regretted not just saying he had to go to the washroom or something.

"...Are you going somewhere?" Moguzo asked.

"Huh? I'm not going anywhere. Just...outside...to get some fresh air?"

Haruhiro just said whatever came into his mind, and it felt kind of awkward, but Moguzo didn't push the matter any further.

"...Okay."

Haruhiro was relieved. "Yeah. Moguzo, you must be tired. You sound it, at least. You should sleep. Good night."

"Good night."

After leaving the room, he debated whether to actually go out for some fresh air. He wouldn't have minded it, but he didn't especially want to, either. If Moguzo was willing to talk with him, maybe he hadn't even needed to leave the room.

Should I have asked Moguzo to give me some advice?

I couldn't do that, could I?

Why couldn't he? He felt like he could explain it, but also like he couldn't. It was just...he couldn't talk to Moguzo.

Moguzo's a good guy, though. He seems like he could keep his mouth shut. But that's not really the issue.

Haruhiro crouched down, leaning his back against the wall in the first floor corridor of the lodging house. There were a number of old lamps in the corridor and, while it couldn't be called bright, it wasn't pitch black.

Now as for whether he could've talked with anyone other than Moguzo, that wasn't really the case. Like, Ranta, never, no way. He wouldn't even consider it. If he talked with Yume, the conversation felt like it would go off into another dimension and make no sense to him. As for Shihoru—

Hmm... Now that I think about it, I've never spoken at length with her, have I? It was hard to imagine a situation where he'd be talking with Shihoru alone.

Now Merry, she'd surely listen to Haruhiro.

But, was that okay? It didn't feel like it. He didn't want to make Merry indulge him anymore. He didn't want to show her his weaknesses, he wanted to act cool—he had those sorts of feelings, but there was more to it than that.

Merry joined the party after it'd already been formed, so while it's not quite that she feels less of a member than any of us, she's more enthusiastic about it, you could say, like she feels she needs to contribute to the party, I think. I feel like I'd be taking advantage of that, and that makes me hesitant. I may be overthinking it, though.

Besides, what did he need to worry so much over?

After getting through a life and death crisis through sheer luck, they were doing pretty well now. True, if their luck had been bad, they could've been wiped out. However, running into Death Spots at that particular time had been bad luck, too, and it had been Haruhiro's good luck that'd let him kill it. It all balanced out.

In the end, Haruhiro may just have been dissatisfied.

He was thinking so hard about the party. With desperation and sincerity, he was wracking his brains and agonizing. Yet, what of his comrades? They were taking it pretty easy. They were learning new skills, procuring new equipment, and feeling like they'd become stronger by doing so.

Well, actually, they might've been getting stronger, but even so, Haruhiro and his group were the lowest level of volunteer soldiers. It was no time to be getting full of himself just because Kemuri of the Day Breakers had treated them to a round after he'd killed Death Spots. That hadn't been skill; it'd been purely that he'd been blessed with good luck. He had to make sure he didn't draw the wrong conclusions from it. Why didn't the rest of them get that? Was Haruhiro the only one who understood? Were things okay like this?

If we get carried away with ourselves, that's dangerous.

Bad things always happen.

Everyone should know that very well by now.

And yet...

"...Ah... Geez." Haruhiro pulled at his hair.

This is getting to be too much trouble.

All this muddled thinking isn't going to change anything. If everyone else is fine with things, then maybe it's fine.

When he went to stand up, he heard a noise. Or, rather, he heard footsteps. Someone was walking this way.

They were coming from the entrance hall.

In the lamplight, he saw them. Two people. Both of them girls. Not Yume and Shihoru. The new volunteer soldiers, then?

He knew that there were new people who had become volunteer soldier trainees after them. He'd gone for a bath at close to the same time as two or three of the guys, so they'd spoken briefly, but he hadn't even met the girls yet.

Maybe I should go back to the room?

But Haruhiro didn't move. Because they were girls? Because he at least wanted to check out if they were cute or not? Because he was hoping he might get acquainted with them, that they'd become close? He couldn't say that he was completely free of those ulterior motives, but he couldn't say for sure that he had them, either.

Well, I'll just sort of see what happens.

Haruhiro stayed crouching where he was. He tried not to look in their direction. Though, if he kept looking down, that'd seem forced. He was looking at the wall, without staring off into space. That was how he was trying to look.

Am I an idiot? What am I doing? They must be wondering who this weird guy is. It's showing in the way they walk. They're clearly on guard.

It's fine, I'm harmless, Haruhiro thought to himself. *I won't do anything, okay? Go on, go on. Don't you mind me.*

He should've left before the girls came.

It's weird, isn't it? I'm finding my own actions suspicious. It happens, I guess. Sometimes. I dunno. Does it? Hmm.

The girls walked in front of Haruhiro.

Then, one of them stopped.

Somehow...

Huh?

It feels like...someone's looking at me?

Haruhiro raised his face and looked towards the girls. He hadn't been imagining it.

A girl with her hair cut in a bob was staring at Haruhiro with her big eyes.

Her eyes really were big. They looked like they might fall out at any moment.

She had slight bags forming under her eyes. Her pouty lips gave her a moody appearance, and she gave off an impression of being hard to approach. Yet, on the other hand, he was strangely interested in her.

Hold on, this girl, why is she staring at me like this?

"Choco?" the other, short-haired girl said, placing a hand on the girl with the bob cut's shoulder. "Is something up?"

"Huh—" The one who had spoken without intending to wasn't the bob cut girl, it was Haruhiro. "...Choco?"

Choco.

Did she say Choco?

"Yes?" the bob cut girl asked, tilting her head to the side.

I was crouched down in front of some big box full of light.

There was someone standing next to me. A girl with her hair in a bob.
...Choco.

That was what I called the girl with the bob cut.

...What was that?

Just now.

I was remembering...? I remembered? I dunno. But. Choco.

Choco.

That name at least, I remember. Just the name? No. That's not it.

Those big eyes. The slight bags underneath them. Those pouty lips. Her hairstyle. That bob cut.

I know her.

"Uh, hey."

But what should I say to her?

"Do you know me?" Like that? If she did, she would be acting like it. This doesn't feel like a meeting between old acquaintances.

But, she was looking at Haruhiro. Everyone had forgotten what'd happened to them before coming to Grimgar. Maybe she'd forgotten, too, but there was something tugging at the back of her mind. Like there was for Haruhiro. If so...

The short haired girl stepped between her and Haruhiro. "...If you're here, you must be a volunteer soldier, too, right? Did you need something from us?'

"No, it's not that I need anything."

"Well, goodbye, then."

"Ah... Right."

"Let's go, Choco."

"Okay."

They walked off quickly.

As they did, Choco turned back just once. Their eyes met. However, she soon turned away again.

Did they think I'm creepy?

If so, it's a bit of a shock. No, not just a bit. It might be a major shock.

"...Choco," Haruhiro whispered, and then thought, *If she could hear me, she'd be even more creeped out.*

Is she that same Choco?

"It's a coincidence...right?"

3. A Story of Impossible Dreams

"Heyyyyyy! Waaaaake uuuuuup!"

"Gwah?!" Haruhiro shouted.

What?! What happened?! An incident? An accident? A natural disaster? A manmade disaster?

It was an elbow.

Haruhiro was shocked into awareness when Ranta, the stupid jerk, elbowed him hard in the solar plexus.

"...Wh-what was that for, out of nowhere?! What the hell, man! Don't do that! I can only tolerate so much of your crap!" he shouted.

"Huhhh? What're you so mad about, Haruhiro?" Ranta asked. "You were sleeping the day away, so I decided to be a nice guy and gently wake you up, you know?"

"I couldn't get to sleep last night! Is there something wrong with that?!"

"Yeah, there is! That's why I'm saying something about it, duh!" Ranta said.

"What could possibly be wrong with it?!" Haruhiro demanded.

"When I went to the trouble of rushing back here to give you the extra special info I heard, you were snoring like a baby, that's what's wrong!"

"U-um, Ranta-kun..." Moguzo began.

"Shove off, Moguzo! You just stay quiet! This is between me and Haruhiro! Until it's settled, neither of us can move on! This is about setting things right between us, as men! Hey, Haruhiro! Right here, right now, we'll settle this!"

"...Settle what?" Haruhiro asked.

"Huh?! You know what! That thing! Uh, basically... What was it again?"

"How should I know?" Haruhiro sighed, sitting up. Every time he moved, his upper bunk bed creaked. Looking up, he saw the familiar ceiling of the volunteer soldier lodging house.

"So," Haruhiro reluctantly turned to face Ranta. "What's this extra special info?"

"Right, that!" Ranta grinned.

What an incredibly aggravating expression. How can he manage to piss people off so badly with a simple grin? It's practically a talent.

Of course, it's the worst, most awful talent ever.

"You didn't wake up at the usual time, and Moguzo said something stupid about waiting and letting you wake up on your own, so there I was, feeling real hungry, and so I went to the bakery. Yeah, the bakery. You know where I mean? Tattan's Bakery, just outside of West Town. Well, when I did, there were a bunch of volunteer soldiers there. They were talking about it. Now, I'll bet you want to ask what 'it' was, right? Well, hold your horses. There's a proper order, a sequence, to all this. It's like that in dating, too, isn't it? Oh, maybe it's too soon for you to understand that. You're still just a little kid, after all. I mean, it's *pretty* obvious that you're still a virgin. Not me, of course. I'm the *king* of the old in and out. It's like they say, experienced candidates receive preferential treatment. You get me? With my incredible technique, I leave those she-cats in an ecstatic frenzy."

"...Okay, could you just let me know how long I'll need to listen to your nonsense before you get to the point?" Haruhiro asked.

"It's not nonsense," Ranta insisted. "The only thing that comes out of my mouth is truth. In other words, it's all fact."

"So, what's the extra special info?" Haruhiro asked.

"Before that, man, get down here. It's extremely unpleasant having to look up to talk to a guy who I feel is beneath me."

Yes, it was a bunk bed, but it wasn't *that* high. The top level was at shoulder level for Ranta, who was standing on the floor. But, with Haruhiro sitting up in bed, he was looking down at Ranta. It may not have felt especially good doing so, but it didn't feel bad either.

"I don't wanna."

"How about you try dying then? Huh?" Ranta exploded.

"...Man, you whine about every little thing," Haruhiro muttered.

"Huh? Did you just say something?"

"Yeah, I did," Haruhiro said in irritation. "I said you're a like a pesky insect. Ah. Sorry. That's not it. I said you *are* a pesky insect."

"You dolt! I'm not a pesky insect, I'm a beneficial one!"

"What, you don't mind being an insect?"

"Huh...?"

Tired of the fruitless squabbling, Haruhiro got down from his bunk, taking a seat on the frame of the lower bunk.

"So? What's the extra special info?" he asked. "—Hold on, how many times am I going to have to ask that same question before I get an answer?"

"Don't try to get things without working for them," Ranta said. "I sound like an old man now!"

"Hah, hahaha..." Moguzo laughed, causing Ranta to crack a smile.

"You get it, Moguzo. Unlike Haruhiro here. You get what makes a gag funny. Haruhiro's hopeless. He doesn't get a thing. He doesn't have a single funny bone in his body!"

Haruhiro did his best to clear away the murky feelings that were beginning to cloud his heart. "So? What's the extra special info?"

"You're repeating yourself, Haruhiro-kuuuun," Ranta said.

"So? What's the extra special info?"

"Oh! There it is again! You're trying hard now."

"Out with it!" Haruhiro leapt up, grabbed Ranta by the throat and started to throttle him. "Tell me! Just say it already! While I'm still holding back!"

"Y-you're not holding back...! Ow! That hurts! Sto—are you trying to *kill* me?! Fine! I'll talk! I'll talk, okay! Okay?! It's an order! There's an order!"

"An order...?" Haruhiro exchanged glances with Moguzo.

Moguzo's stomach grumbled. His face turned a deep shade of red. "Ah. S-sorry. I'm hungry..."

"No, it's nothing to be sorry for," Haruhiro said. "You can't stop yourself from getting hungry. Look, we just so happen to have some bread here, so why not eat?"

"I bought that, and you know it!" Ranta snapped. "At Tattan's Bakery, the cheap place near West Town! I bought the bread, so it's all mine!"

Ranta was being a cheapskate, so Haruhiro and Moguzo decided to go get breakfast. Maybe he didn't want to be left alone, because Ranta tagged along, snacking on bread. Along the way, he explained what an order was, acting as if the knowledge made him important somehow.

According to Ranta, orders were issued for volunteer soldiers by the Alterna Frontier Volunteer Army Corps, Red Moon. However, despite being called orders, nobody was required to follow them. Volunteer soldiers decided for themselves whether to accept or not. That said, if someone suitable for the job chose not to accept without good reason, it did tend to cause other volunteer soldiers to look down on them.

Well, that just meant that, if there was an order it looked like they could handle, it was best to just shut up and take care of it quickly.

Of course, there was a more concrete reason why they'd want to accept an order.

Money.

The reward for an order consisted of an advance payment and another payment on completion. As soon as they accepted an order, a volunteer soldier could collect the advance. The rest would be paid out if and when the task was successfully completed.

If they pocketed the advance, but then didn't work on the order, there'd be a fine. If the volunteer soldier in question was judged to have acted maliciously, they'd be summoned to the volunteer soldier corps office. If they didn't respond to the summons, a bounty would be placed on their head, making them a target for bounty hunters.

Incidentally, the work of capturing bounties was treated like an order. Sometimes, there'd be bounties placed on criminals or dishonest merchants, and there were some volunteer soldiers who preferred the bounty hunter-like work of pursuing these targets.

The compensation for orders came not as cash, but as a military payment certificate used by the Frontier Army. These were called military scrip, and were thin chits made of copper. Basically, they were paid with a promissory note. Military scrips could be exchanged for cash at the Yorozu Deposit Company, or they could be used in place of money at businesses that had a contract with the Frontier Army or Volunteer Soldier Corps.

While Ranta was explaining all this, Haruhiro and Moguzo decided to go to the food stall village near the craftsmen's town to eat a noodle dish called soruzo.

The stall village was busy with craftspeople even early in the morning, and at this time of day, it was even more lively than the marketplace in the northern district. Soruzo was a dish of meat thrown into a salty broth along with yellow noodles made from wheat flour. Haruhiro hadn't thought it was that good at first, but it felt strangely familiar to him, and so he came to eat it sometimes. Having eaten it for a while, he'd gotten hooked on the stuff, and now it felt really tasty to him.

As Haruhiro and Moguzo were blowing on their noodles to cool them, Ranta, who'd been munching away at his bread, finally gave in to temptation and ordered a bowl, too.

"Yum...! This's the stuff! It's so good! Soruzo's awesome!"

"Oh, come on, you're exaggerating... Also, your nose is running, Ranta," Haruhiro said.

"Of course it's running! It's gonna run like crazy! Haruhiro! Don't you get it?! This soruzo, it's perfect!"

"S-soruzo's delicious, huh," Moguzo said, already starting on his second bowl. No—

"...Moguzo, correct me if I'm wrong, but is that your second—no, *third*, bowl?" Haruhiro asked.

"Y-yeah. It's easy to eat, you know, so I just keep wolfing it down faster and faster..."

"Gwahahaha!" Ranta laughed. "Nice work, Moguzo! You're not my rival for nothing! But...I'm going for it, too! On to the second bowl! Pops! Hit me with another one!"

"Coming up!"

"Well, it's fine if you want to..." Haruhiro scooped up the noodles with his wooden fork and slowly carried them to his mouth.

Okay, sure, they're delicious. But, it's morning. I can't wolf down food like that. It'd be too heavy for my stomach.

"Still, though, Moguzo, this is delicious and all," Ranta said, "but, you know what? If we tried to make it ourselves, I bet we could, don't you think? Well?"

"Huh...? Ah, yeah, uh... I'm not so sure...? The soup might be a bit hard..."

"No, man, we could do it," said Ranta. "This stuff is easy. You just throw a bunch of ingredients in a pot. Just boil that, and it'll come out tasting all right, I'm sure."

"No...I don't think it's that simple...you know?"

"You think? It feels like we could pull it off. What's in this soup?"

"Let's see, probably chicken bones...pork fat, too, maybe. Then there're the vegetables—there're onions and carrots in here."

"Oh? Good job figuring all that out, Moguzo. Me, I had no clue, you know?"

"...I'm amazed you said you could make it, then," Haruhiro took a shot at Ranta, but he got ignored, as expected.

I'm fine with that, Haruhiro told himself. *Really.*

Moguzo brought his bowl to his lips and drank the soup, his brow furrowing. "...Yeah. If you add garlic, and maybe ginger...it might give it a more satisfying flavor."

"Ohh? Ohhh?!" Ranta exclaimed. "Moguzo, buddy, we could do it, don't you think? Once we make some money, what say you and me open a restaurant?!"

"Ah, ha ha ha... But, we're volunteer soldiers and all..."

"Buddy, don't sweat the small stuff like that!" Ranta declared. "If we're bringing in money, it doesn't matter what job we're doing. Besides, it's not like we can stay in that violent world for the rest of our lives. Eventually, we'll retire, and then we'll need to start a second career. You know what that is? A second career. It's a second, uh, you know. What is it? Um, it's a second...career, yeah."

"You just said the same thing again," Haruhiro said helpfully.

"Shut up, Haruhiro. Just shut up. Seriously. Seriously. You can get lost! I'm having an important talk with Moguzo here! Anyway, how about it, Moguzo? Want to do that with me? Ranta and Moguzo's Soruzo Shop. We'll split the profits seventy to me, thirty to you...is what I'd *like* to say, but I'm fine with splitting it fifty-fifty. We'll start studying now, so we'll be ready when the time comes. How about it? Hm?"

"A restaurant, huh?" Moguzo looked like he wasn't entirely against the idea. "It could be nice. Doing something like that. Compared to fighting...well, it seems easier at least. I'll think about it."

"Yeah! You think about it! Be super positive about it! We're gonna make so much money! Hand over fist! We'll open a whole chain of restaurants! First, we start with ten locations in Alterna! Our goal will be 1,700 across all of Grimgar! You and I could do it, too! Well, that's a long way off, though!" Ranta noisily slurped his soruzo soup, then let out a stinky, satisfied belch. "So! Finally, I think it's time for me to talk about the order! Are you mentally prepared? Am I good to start? I am, right? Don't you tell me otherwise at this late stage of the game."

"You're being seriously annoying, so just tell us already..." Haruhiro muttered.

"Haaaaruhiroooo! When you call people annoying, you're being one hundred! Nay! One thousand, ten thousand, no, no, no, five hundred million times as annoying! Get that through your head already!"

"Yeah, yeah."

"You only need to say 'yeah' one hundred times," said Ranta.

"Yeah—Wait, not one time. One hundred times?! That's too many!"

"Don't underestimate me! Brilliantly surprising people is what I, Ranta-sama, do!"

"...Even Moguzo's laughing," Haruhiro said.

"S-sorry," Moguzo murmured. "It's just, that one was funny..."

"Moooguzoooo! What do you mean 'that one'?! It's not just that one, it's all the ones! I'm always funny! The wandering comedian king, Rantaman, that's what they call me! If you doubt my one-in-a-hundred sense of humor, even if you're my future business partner, I'm not going to be able to forgive you!"

"One-in-a-hundred?" Haruhiro asked. "That doesn't feel like anything special to me."

"Haaaaruhiiiiro-kuuuun..." Ranta said.

"...What's with that way of saying my name? It's kind of creepy."

"I meant to say one-in-a-hundred-million, but I accidentally only said one-in-a-hundred, yeeees. Do you get it noooow?"

"Well, if so, that's fine. Now tell us about the order. This is going nowhere."

"That's *your* fault!" Ranta shouted.

"Don't try to turn this on me, like I'm the bad guy..."

"You *are* the bad guy!"

"Enough already, just talk! What is it, this current order?!" Haruhiro snapped.

"Mwahahahahaha! Don't let this shock you, okay?!" Ranta suddenly stood up, wiggling both his arms, imitating...snakes? Or something... "It's this!"

"...No, there's no way I'm going to be able to figure it out from that," Haruhiro said.

"It's a two-headed snake!" Ranta had his right-hand snake turn and say hello to his left-hand snake. "The operation to retake Deadhead Watching Keep and Riverside Iron Fortress, code name: 'Two-Headed Snake'! Participating in this operation, let it be no secret, is the order! Well, the deadline for going to Riversides's already passed, and they say that one's a job for experienced teams, so if we're going to take part, it'll be Deadhead we go to. The upfront pay is twenty silver, with eighty more on completion, making one gold altogether! That's a solid gold coin! And that's for each of us, you know?! That's incredible!"

Moguzo's eyes went wide, and he let out an "Oooh..."

"One gold coin..." Haruhiro thought that was a lot. But, at the same time, he remembered that when they'd lost a comrade, Renji had come over to him and said, "Consolation money. Take it." and thrown him a gold coin.

Renji sure is rich, huh, Haruhiro thought, even though it was silly to dwell on it.

"Now, Deadhead," Ranta said, sitting back in his chair, "is here." He pointed to a spot on the table. "...No, maybe here? Maybe around here? Or could it be around here?"

"Won't any spot do?" Haruhiro asked.

"Well, yeah. But, you know. It's an orc fortress six kilometers north of Alterna. When I say six kilometers, that sounds pretty close. Or, rather, it *is* really close. Of course, our Frontier Army has attacked the fortress many times, and even taken it in the past. However, they can never hold it long. Why do you think that is?"

"Hmm..." Moguzo crossed his arms in thought, tilting his head to the side. "...Because they have no guts...or something? That's not it, huh..."

"Of course it isn't! No, no! The answer is, right around here..." Ranta pointed to a spot near the edge of the table. "Riverside Iron Fortress. This fortress, it's about forty kilometers west of Deadhead, on the bank of a jet river, and if you go further upstream, you'll run into the territory of the former Kingdom of Nananka. You know what that is? No, I bet you don't. The former Kingdom of Nananka. It means orcs, man, orcs! Nowadays, there's a country full of orcs there. So, they're able to travel by boat and carry in supplies and troops. Deadhead's a teeny-tiny little keep, but when the Frontier Army attacks, they raise smoke signals, or something. When they do that, reinforcements get sent in from Riverside immediately."

Haruhiro furrowed his brow. "But it's a full forty kilometers away."

"The orcish army's got what they call dragoons," Ranta said, taking on a funny pose.

Is that supposed to be some sort of animal? An octopus? No.

"They're called dragoons, but they don't ride dragons, they ride these huge lizards," Ranta said. "The big lizards are called horse-dragons. They're crazy fast, and they can make the trek from Riverside to Deadhead in as little as an hour."

"Ah," Moguzo punched his right fist into the palm of his left hand. "Is that why we're doing both at the same time?"

"Clever thinking, just what I'd expect from my business partner." Ranta tried to snap his fingers, but they didn't make a sound. He tried again a few times, but he just couldn't get it to work.

Looks like he finally gave up.

"...Dammit," Ranta muttered. "Curse you, dry skin."

Haruhiro sighed. "Don't try to blame your skin..."

"Don't butt in on everything, even me blaming my skin! What are you, my mother-in-law?!"

"So, moving on... Where were we?" Haruhiro asked.

"Ignoring me, huh?! You've got guts, pal!"

"Riverside Iron Fortress, was it?" Haruhiro asked. "And Deadhead Watching Keep, they're attacking them together... Wait, somehow, that almost seems like a war, don't you think?"

"...Tch. You just insist on ignoring me. Haruhiro, didn't you know? We humans have been at war with the orcs, the undead, and more, all this time."

"Well, I had a sort of vague sense of that. But we didn't seem to be going at it that hard, you know."

"When the chance comes along, we go at it hard," Ranta said. "Not that long ago, a bunch of orcs fought their way into Alterna, remember?"

"Ah... Ish Dogran? Was that it? The guy Renji killed."

"Yeah, that's it. Apparently, this got started as revenge for that. That's what got it going. And so, if we're going to do it, rather than just harass them, we might as well take the whole fortress good and proper, that's my thinking. We've taken Deadhead a number of times in the past, but they always take it back from us in no time. It's Riverside that's to blame for that. So, we're not making the same mistake again."

Ranta talks about it with a condescending tone, like "The Frontier Army's learned from their mistakes, wahahaha," but the more I hear, the more clear it is that this is a war.

"...Isn't it kinda dangerous?" Haruhiro asked. "And, hold on, we're not attacking with just volunteer soldiers... There's no way that'd be it, right?"

"Obviously, the Frontier Army will accompany us, or rather, they're the main force and we'll be accompanying them," Ranta snorted. "The volunteer soldiers are there in a supporting role, of course. Try to think a little. Are you a moron? Don't just keep looking at it with sleepy eyes like that, Haruhirion."

"Don't talk about my eyes. I'll stab you from behind. Also, drop the Haruhirion thing."

"Haruhirion can't take a joke, I see."

"Come *on*, man..."

"U-um," Moguzo interrupted them. "H-how many people will be going to do that...? Like, numbers?"

"Numbers?" Ranta stroked his chin with his thumb. "Let's see, at

Deadhead there'll be five or six hundred from the Frontier Army, they were saying. As for volunteer soldiers, it was one hundred, maybe a hundred and fifty. Riverside's one tough fortress, so I expect it'll turn into a pretty intense battle. I hear Soma's Day Breakers, 'Red Devil' Ducky's Berserkers, 'One-on-One' Max's Iron Knuckle, and Shinohara's Orion will be participating there. Honestly, that's some crazy stuff. 'If you aren't confident in your skills,' it feels like they're saying, 'if you come, you're gonna die, so don't come, you'll only get in the way.'"

I feel like I understand why Ranta's acting like this'll be easy, Haruhiro thought. *Ranta's taking it too lightly, that's gotta be it. He thinks taking Riverside Iron Fortress will be hard, but Deadhead Watching Keep will fall easily. Actually, he probably thinks we'll win the moment we start the attack.*

"So, there you have it." Ranta had both his hand-snakes make bitey motions. "One gold coin! We've gotta do it, with that up for grabs! It's decided! Yup! Let's go and apply already! There're three days left before the deadline, but you know that proverb about striking while the iron's hot, right? Or is it an idiom? Well, whichever, it's a thing they say, and I say I'll go to the office right now and—"

"Y-you can't do that," Moguzo said, stopping Ranta before Haruhiro had the chance. "...W-we've got to let everyone else weigh in on it first..."

"Wahhh? Who cares about doing that? Just be like, 'We're doing this, okay, let's go,' and they'll tag right along. They won't even realize what's up, not those girls!"

"You can't be right about that..." Haruhiro said, scratching his head. "Well, I'll bring it up with them tonight, and we can make a decision after that. There's still time, so it should be fine."

Ranta snorted. "Oh, fine, if you insist."

Next time, I'm going to punch him. Haruhiro promised himself that.

Grimgar of Fantasy and Ash

4. Don't Go With The Flow

After a day of work in the Cyrene Mines, the party sold off their loot, grabbed dinner, and then all rushed in to Sherry's Tavern.

"Of course, I'm getting beer, like a real man should," Ranta declared.

"Well, m-me, too, then," Moguzo added.

"I'll get mead," said Haruhiro.

"Ah, me, too," said Merry.

"Yume thinks she'll go with lemonade. It's so bubbly and delicious."

"...I'll go with that, too," Shihoru nodded.

Soon after, the drinks came around. Ranta took it upon himself to start running the show.

"Okay, everyone got theirs?! Good work today! Cheers...!"

"G-good work today!" Moguzo said.

"Good work," Haruhiro agreed.

"Good work, everyone," said Merry.

"Good worky-worky-work," said Yume.

"...Good work," Shihoru added.

Ranta and Moguzo both tilted back their beers and chugged.

Moguzo was probably just doing it because he was parched, while Ranta didn't want to lose to Moguzo.

Haruhiro, sipping away at his slightly tangy, but sweet, mead, couldn't understand it at all. *What the hell? Why is he so competitive?*

"Bwahh! I...win...!" Ranta slammed his empty ceramic mug down on the table.

What're you going to do if it breaks? Haruhiro wondered.

"Moguzo! How do you like that? I won! Wahahahahahahahaha!"

"Uh...sure," Moguzo said, putting down his mug without finishing it. "Y-you're amazing, Ranta-kun. Drinking it all in one go like that."

"I know, right? I *am* awesome, aren't I? You really do get it, Moguzo," Ranta said proudly. "I should've expected no less from my future business partner."

Yume blinked repeatedly. "Blinking partner?"

"No, a business partner..." Haruhiro at least made the effort to correct her. "And, hold on, what kind of partner would that even be? A 'blinking partner'..."

Suddenly, Shihoru let out a strange "Hic." When they looked over, Shihoru was covering her mouth with both hands and looking down. Her face was a little red.

"What's wrong, Shihoru?" Haruhiro asked.

"...I-it's nothing... Nothing, really..." she murmured.

"Oh, yeah," Ranta displayed one of his irritating grins. "Shihoru. I'll bet you were imagining something weird."

"...S-something weird...?"

"I don't know what it'd have been. I'm not equipped with a delusion engine as powerful as yours, you know?"

"I-I don't have an engine like that...!"

"So, that means I don't have the same delusion energy coursing through me that you do, get it?" Ranta went on.

"It's not coursing through me...!"

"That's some nasty accusation, Ranta!" Yume said, holding Shihoru close to her. "Shihoru's not like that. She doesn't have no delugin' apogee, or whatever weird thing you said, got it!"

"...You got the words wrong, though," Merry whispered quietly.

"Whuh?! Did Yume goof it up again?!"

Ranta laughed, mockingly. "Your words are wrong way too often, you know that! It drives the people listening to you crazy, so don't talk for a while! Shut up!"

"Nuh-uh, no way!" Yume shot back.

"You don't get the right to refuse here!"

"Yume has her own opinion, too!"

"No one said anything about you having an opinion or not!"

"Ranta, *you* did!"

"I said you don't have the right to refuse! Right! To! Re-fuse! You know what that is?! The right to refuse!"

"Yume knows that much!"

"Yeah, well, before we talk about what you do or don't know, stop getting words wrong so often! Do you have holes for ears?!" Ranta shouted.

"Ranta." Haruhiro stuck his fingers in his ears. "Yep, they're there. Holes in my ears. Everyone has holes for ears. Or are you blind? Do you have holes for eyes?"

"Huh...?" Ranta realized his mistake, but that wasn't enough to make him change his attitude. He gave it a sarcastic shrug. "—Here we go again. This is it. This here. This is the problem with our party's leader. He likes to pick at any little mistake people make! On top of that, the way he criticizes them for it is downright malicious! What an awful personality!"

"You're the last one I want to hear that from..." Haruhiro muttered.

"If you don't want to hear it, then don't act in a way that makes me say it, huh? Show some restraint, okay?"

"...Hey, Moguzo," Haruhiro said. "Listen, just a friendly word of warning, but if you're planning to run a business with *this* piece of shit in the future, you really ought to reconsider. There's no way it'll be a success."

Moguzo laughed awkwardly.

"A business?" Merry asked, cocking her head to the side.

"Ohhh." Haruhiro told her about what'd happened at the food stall. "...So, once they've saved up some money and retired from being volunteer soldiers, Ranta suggested to Moguzo that they open up a soruzo shop together, you see."

"Ohh," Yume mumbled. "Soruzo, that's that stuff that's like ramen, huh?"

"Ramen..." For an instant, Haruhiro felt a salty taste spread through his mouth.

Ranta crossed his arms in thought. "...Ramen."

"Ramen..." Shihoru touched her lips.

Moguzo leaned out over the table. "...Ramen."

"Ramen—Wait..." Merry said, a slightly frustrated look on her face. "What was that again?"

"Whut?" Yume looked around restlessly. "Ramen is... Um... Huh? That's odd. Yume, did she know it...from somewhere? Maybe? What was it again? Huh? What was Yume talking about with everyone again?"

Haruhiro scratched his head. "...What *were* we talking about?"

"About ramen," Moguzo said in a strong tone. "We were talking about ramen. We... We probably know what ramen is. That's right. Soruzo, it's kind of like ramen. When I first ate it, I thought it tasted like something. It was ramen I was thinking of. I couldn't remember it at the time. I wonder why not. I've always loved ramen. Ranta-kun."

"Huh? Oh...?" Ranta asked.

"Someday, let's do it. Open a restaurant."

"Huh?"

"But, me, I don't want to open a soruzo place, I want to make ramen. I'll save up money, study, and when I can make ramen that tastes just right, let's do it, let's open that restaurant."

"A restaurant..." Ranta grinned broadly, grabbing Moguzo around the shoulder. Even though it was Ranta, this was a smile that wasn't infuriating to see. "Yeah! You'll be in charge of the cooking and raising capital! Leave everything else to me! I swear I'll lead us to success!"

"Yeah!"

"...The cooking is fine, but raising capital, too...?" Haruhiro muttered. *What, aren't you putting in any money yourself?* Haruhiro wanted to add, but he'd have felt bad doing so after seeing how excited Moguzo was about doing it. *I can warn him any time. I don't need to be a killjoy right here and now.*

Either way, it was a long way off. Probably an astonishingly long way off.

The saying about the best-laid plans of mice and men came to mind, but Haruhiro wasn't so boorish that he was going to tell them to stop talking about it. He felt things were fine the way they were.

Honestly, he was even a little jealous.

Haruhiro was only ever thinking about tomorrow, maybe three days into the future at most. Even if he wanted to think about more than that, he couldn't.

And, technically, he had something he needed to make a decision on within those three days that was the most he could think about, anyway.

"By the way, since everyone's here, I had something I wanted to talk about," Haruhiro said.

When Haruhiro gave them a quick rundown of the order—

"Hell! Yeah!" Ranta cried, thrusting a fist into the air so hard it seemed like he might jump up on top of his chair. "We've gotta do it! That goes without saying, I mean! It's a gold coin! Golden work! Not doing it isn't an option! What're we gonna do if we don't?!"

"...Hrmm..." Shihoru looked down, clearly not enthusiastic about the idea.

Yeah, that figures, Haruhiro thought. *I mean, it's Shihoru. How does Merry feel?*

She was lowering her eyes, stroking her chin, looking like she was deep in thought, but she hadn't approved of it yet, either. She probably planned to go along with the rest of them. She might be trying to be considerate.

Everything up to this point was going as Haruhiro had expected.

"Yume, yeah," Yume puffed up her cheeks, looking up and away diagonally. "She doesn't care either way, maybe?"

"...Oh. Is that right?" Harurhiro asked.

"Hm? What?"

"Oh, it's nothing."

If Ranta said he wanted to do something, Yume would usually oppose it. That was the way it usually went, but it looked like things were different this time. Why? If anything, Haruhiro wanted to ask that, but if he did something that'd encourage conflict between Yume and Ranta, that wouldn't be very mature, and he didn't feel it'd be right for the party leader to do that, either. Even if Ranta was a hopeless case, he was still a comrade, and it was best not to rock the boat.

But, wait, hold on?

That meant that Haruhiro was against, Ranta was for, Shihoru was weakly against, Merry was neutral, Yume was neutral, too...

"I..." Moguzo looked more serious than ever.

Somehow, that gave Haruhiro a bad feeling. That bad feeling was right.

"I'd like to try it...maybe?" said Moguzo.

"Moguzoooo!" Ranta thrust his fist out at Moguzo. "Yeah!"

"Y-yeah...?" Moguzo asked.

"Get over here! Say, yeah! Yeah!"

"...Y-yeah?"

When Moguzo hesitantly bumped his fist into Ranta's, Ranta said "Yeah," and bumped his fist back, then he bumped their forearms, then elbows together, saying "Yeah," finally finishing by locking their arms together firmly.

"Wahahahaha! Seriously! Seriously! That's my future business partner for you! We're both frontliners, too! It's no exaggeration to call him my partner! We're like peas in a pod, Moguzo! Don't you think so?! You do, right?!" Ranta shouted.

"Ah! Er, yeah. Y-you're right. Ha ha ha..."

"Good, good, good, good! Hey, Haruhiro!"

"Huh? Wh-what?"

"Majority vote." Ranta put his arm around Moguzo's shoulders, licking his lips. He had a look in his eyes like a carnivore about to devour its prey. "Go on, let's take a vote."

"No..." Haruhiro said.

Wait, wait, wait.

Hold on.

This is no good. It's bad. I don't like where this is going.

If Moguzo was voting for, then along with Ranta's vote there were two fors. Haruhiro would vote against, and probably Shihoru as well, giving them two. Merry and Yume's two votes remained unclear.

If it comes down to it, I feel like Yume will follow me, Haruhiro thought. *But, when I ask myself if that's guaranteed—I dunno. Now that Moguzo's sided with Ranta, I can't be confident.*

"Ah—" Haruhiro started to speak, but then looked to Merry and Yume, sizing them up.

Man.

Which is it? Are the two of them for? Or against?

I don't know.

"Let's do it tomorrow," he said.

"Huhhhhhhhhh...?!" Ranta's eyes went wide. "What do you mean tomorrow, you idiot?! Don't put off until tomorrow what can be done today! Are you a sloth?!"

"...It's fine," Haruhiro said. "We don't have to rush. There's still time before the deadline. We can take a day to think it over properly, and it still won't be too late to decide then."

Merry raised her hand to support him. "I think that's a good idea."

She's like a goddess. She looks positively radiant. Oh, I guess she's always like that.

"Well..." Yume lay down on the table. She'd only drunk non-alcoholic lemonade, but she was acting tipsy. "Yume agrees with Merry, maybe. It should be fine, no?"

"...Y-yeah," Shihoru nodded. "...It's a good idea. I think so, too."

It didn't look like Moguzo had any objections. "Yeah, you're right. It's fine. There's no rush."

"You people...!" Ranta screamed.

Ranta can hardly contain himself, but who cares about him. For now, it looks like I can get through this. Haruhiro breathed a sigh of relief, looking around the tavern.

Sherry's had the same crowd as usual. In other words, it was packed with volunteer soldiers.

Among them, there should've been a good number who'd already accepted the order and would be participating in Operation Two-Headed Snake. *It might be a good idea to gather information,* Haruhiro thought.

"...I'm not so good at doing this kind of stuff," he murmured.

Honestly, I'd rather not talk to strangers. I can't afford to be saying that now, I know, but still.

Grimgar
of
Fantasy and Ash

5. That's What it Feels Like

I understand that, so I tried my hardest, you know...? Haruhiro thought. *Well, as much as I could, at least.*

He'd tried calling out to the senior volunteer soldiers that he'd talked to in the past and asking them about it. The fact that the affable Shinohara and his gang hadn't come to Sherry's hurt his chances a bit—maybe?

Shinohara was usually kind and polite, of course, and so were the other members of Orion. If he were to ask politely, without demanding too much of them, they'd probably tell him what they knew.

Well, outside of Shinohara, the only one Haruhiro could easily talk to was Kikkawa, the guy who'd come to Grimgar at the same as him, but was super easygoing and had a lot of connections.

But Kikkawa wasn't there today, even though Haruhiro met him at Sherry's pretty often. Had he gone off somewhere, maybe?

Despite appearances, Kikkawa was a member of one of the more senior volunteer soldiers, Tokimune's, party, so he'd gotten a lot further than Haruhiro and his group.

Come to think of it, he mentioned something, I think. If I remember correctly, some place called Wonder Hole is their main hunting ground now. That was somewhere in the Quickwind Plains, right? Wonder Hole, huh?

Haruhiro was sitting in the hall on the first floor of the volunteer soldier lodging house, leaning with his back against the wall.

Ranta and Moguzo were back in the room, fast asleep. Maybe it was the alcohol, but they both snored incredibly loudly. Because of that, Haruhiro hadn't been able to sleep—though maybe that was just one of the many usual reasons.

He'd spoken to a handful of senior volunteer soldiers who'd accepted the order, and from what they'd told him, everyone seemed optimistic about their chances of taking Deadhead Watching Keep.

When he asked why, it was apparently because Deadhead had fallen a number of times in past. They could take that keep any time they wanted to. It was just that the reinforcements from Riverside Iron Fortress were hard to deal with, so they usually left it alone.

Even if the volunteer soldiers ignored them, the orcs there hardly ever came to attack Alterna. Even if an incident like the one with Ish Dogran occurred, it wasn't going to shake the fortress city of Alterna. Even in the worst case scenario, if the orcs brought a massive army to attack them, they just had to bar the gates and settle in for a siege.

They had supplies. They could even expect support from the Arabakia Kingdom mainland. Because the orcs knew that too, they never got serious about sending forces after Alterna. The orcish position was that Deadhead was merely a watching keep, and they were monitoring the humans. They didn't station a large force there, so if the humans suddenly attacked, it'd fall easily.

Because that was the general consensus, none of the volunteer soldiers doubted that the mission to take it would succeed. It was a given that they'd win at Deadhead, like they always had up until now. However, since there'd never been a proper attack on Riverside before, nobody knew how that one would go until they tried it.

It seemed like people expected it to go well, though.

After all, it seemed the Frontier Army would be committing a good amount of manpower to taking Riverside, and as for the volunteer soldiers, Soma and his Day Breakers would be participating, along with many other influential clans. It just might work.

That was what most volunteer soldiers seemed to be thinking, and Haruhiro hadn't heard anyone sounding negative about it.

It might be okay to do this...maybe?

After all, it was one gold. One golden coin. Converted to silver, that was one hundred coins.

Recently, Haruhiro and the party had been going to the Cyrene Mines. There'd been times when, on the best days, their daily earnings could exceed thirty silver each. Though, most of the time, it was questionable whether they'd make ten silver each or not. The talismans from elder kobolds like foremen always sold for around five silver at the minimum, so it was fairly stable. However, their living expenses were going up, too. Everyone was clearly eating better than before. They drank, too, and would go out to buy this or that.

From what he'd heard, while the upfront payment and completion bonus were one gold all together, every full night they were out on the mission would earn them another thirty silver each.

That meant, probably, that the higher-ups intended to finish this in a single day.

One gold in one day.

That was a big deal. A *really* big deal.

It was very tempting.

It seemed like a winning battle, and the money was really enticing, so why was Haruhiro so incredibly hesitant?

After leaving Sherry's Tavern, he considered consulting Merry about it. It wasn't something that she always did, but Merry seemed to have a habit of first leaving with everyone else, then turning back and going for another drink by herself.

Haruhiro probably had the opportunity to do it, but he didn't. Why not?

In the bar—no, it wasn't just that—he didn't know when it had started, but lately, Haruhiro had been sensing a wall. It had risen up between Haruhiro and his comrades. Haruhiro was being separated from his comrades by something that felt like a wall.

It must have been his imagination, or rather, he was just overthinking it. It couldn't be that Haruhiro was the only one on this side, and everyone else was on the other side. But, there was a gap between them.

That was a fact.

His comrades were starting to build confidence. In fact, Haruhiro thought that they were growing in strength, too. When they were on the third level of the Cyrene Mines, it was generally pretty easy, after all. That was partially because they no longer needed to worry about Death Spots, but he didn't feel like they could lose. At their current level, if Haruhiro and the others took on a group of seven, no, eight goblins, they could probably handle them now. With kobolds, it'd depend on how many of them there were elders, but usually there were two to three ordinary kobolds for each elder. Even if they went up against three elders and five ordinary kobolds, it wasn't like they couldn't manage that. Not that he wanted to take that sort of risk.

...That's it.

I want to avoid risks as much as possible.

Safety comes first.

As leader, I'm always keeping that in mind.

I don't want us to take any harm. I'd like to keep that to the absolute minimum. If possible, to zero. Actually, zero sounds good. No matter what it takes, I'd like to keep it to zero.

I'm scared. I mean, it's frightening. Everyone else seems calm and composed. Me, not so much. I may not feel like we're going to lose, but I'm always on edge. If we keep thinking, "We can do this, we can do this," I worry we're going to get done in. Eventually, something weird could happen. One of us could mess up horribly. I can't rule the possibility out.

"It's kind of like..." Haruhiro murmured, holding his head in his hands.

Like, you know... I don't believe...in my comrades...? But, even more than that...in myself.

Is that okay? Is it really okay for a guy like me to be the leader?

Haruhiro worried about whether any party with him as leader would be able to keep on going. Though, now, maybe he really was overthinking things?

It wasn't like he'd messed up somehow. *It was just, he felt like he was going to, and he was afraid because of that, that was all. If I were to screw up, then—what if one of my comrades got hurt? What if they died? Those guys, aren't they thinking about that at all? If they aren't, isn't that a little naïve? They're being way too optimistic.*

In the end, that's probably because none of them is the leader. They're not in a position of responsibility, so they can take it easy.

"Ahh..." Haruhiro moaned.

This is getting to be a pain.

It's always like this, though.

Maybe I don't care. I don't need to think too deeply about it. When it comes to the order, just put it to a vote, and if everyone says they want to do it, let them. There's not much else I can do.

"No, no..." Haruhiro shook his head back and forth, still holding it in his hands.

That's no good. I have to care more than that.

"Augh..."

As he was groaning, he heard footsteps, but they immediately stopped. Because he'd been letting out strange noises, whoever the footsteps belonged to might have thought he was crazy and dangerous.

He looked up, and at the other end of the corridor, the girl with her hair in a bob was standing there, pigeon-toed.

"Ah," Haruhiro lowered the hands he'd been holding his head with. "...Erm..."

The girl started to walk towards him. Not slowly and cautiously, as if she were intimidated, but approaching at a leisurely pace.

She was probably going to walk right past him. Well, of course she would. That was obvious, wasn't it? What was she even doing here to begin with? It was past bedtime. He hadn't thought he'd be able to meet her. He hadn't, but maybe, deep down, he'd been hoping he would.

No, it was an exaggeration to say he'd been hoping for it. *I saw her here once before, so maybe I'll meet her here again.* He couldn't deny that the thought had crossed his mind.

Of course, the time being the time, there'd been no guarantee he would meet her. He shouldn't have been able to meet her. She should've walked past Haruhiro. Instead, she stopped. Then, as if after a moment of indecision, she bowed her head to him a little. Then: "... Hey," she said, in an extremely brusque tone.

Depending on the person, that attitude might make someone think she was picking a fight. Even Haruhiro got a little angry.

She's the one who greeted me! She can leave anytime now, and yet she's not going.

The girl made no attempt to make eye contact with Haruhiro. It felt like she wanted to leave, but leaving so soon would be awkward, so she didn't know what to do now.

Though, seriously, you can just go, okay...? Haruhiro thought. He seriously felt that way, but he also wanted to at least talk with her.

Well, not that he'd have had any idea what to talk about. The words weren't coming to him. Nothing even resembling words came out.

"Ha...ha ha ha..." Unable to come up with anything else, he tried laughing a little. The girl gave a little sigh.

Ah, he realized. *She's going to leave.*

"Wait," he said.

"Huh?" She stopped walking. "...What?"

"Nothing..."

Oh, man.

What now? I went and stopped her. My mind's blanked out and gone all white. No way. It can't have gone all white. My face, on the other hand, I'm sure it's ghastly pale.

"W-well... You know. What is it...? Well...um, nothing...really."

"Ah, okay," she said.

"Y-yeah."

"Bye." She turned to leave.

"Ummmm, listen."

"Huh?"

"Huh?!" he yelped.

"Seriously, what?"

"Wh-what? What... I wonder what," he stammered. "Er... Ba... sically, yeah... Uhm..."

Yeah, this is bad. No matter how you look at me, I'm acting like a total weirdo right now, aren't I?

Maybe I should apologize? Say I'm sorry? Would that be weird, too? Too sudden? Would it be bad?

Oh, man, oh, man, oh, man.

"Heh..." She covered her mouth with her sleeve.

Did I just...get laughed at?

With her sleeve still covering the lower half of her face, she said, "You're weird."

"Ah—weird? Am I weird, you think...?" he managed.

"Weird," she said. "And gross."

"No way?!"

"Yes, way."

"Seriously? Augh... This is a huge shock..." he moaned.

"What is it?" She looked back and forth. "What are you doing here?"

"Me? I'm not...doing anything weird, you know? Just being normal, and, well...thinking about some stuff, you could say..." It wasn't funny, but he almost laughed again before he could stop himself. "What about you, Choco?"

"...What, no honorific for me?" she asked, smirking slightly.

"S-sorry. It's just—"

It feels more natural that way. But if I said that, she'd probably be even more creeped out. Really, that's how it is, though. Choco-chan, or Choco-san, maybe—Yeah, no. It's not right. Choco is Choco.

"Are you," Choco narrowed her eyes a little, "a ladies' man? You don't look like it, though."

"...I'm not, okay?" Haruhiro said. "I'm exactly what I look like. I'm not. I'm not a ladies' man at all. Umm, uh—Choco...chan? San?"

"It's fine. Just Choco."

"Ah. Really?"

"Yeah," she said. "Somehow..."

"Somehow, what?"

"...This is going to sound weird, but somehow—You know what, never mind."

"Huh? Tell me," he said. "You've got me wondering."

"I won't say."

"R-really? Well...that's fine."

"So you're fine with it," Choco said.

"Huh?! No, I'm not really fine with it. But you said you wouldn't tell me."

"You weak-willed wussy."

Haruhiro's eyes shot wide open. His heart was beating strangely fast. This wasn't his normal pulse. What was it?

Those words. "You weak-willed wussy." They sound familiar.

Maybe I'm just imagining that. Still, it's not a common thing to call someone—at least, I don't think so.

At least, Haruhiro had never heard the phrase before.

No, that's not true. I have heard it before.

"Choco," he said.

"Yes?" she asked.

"I'll bet you don't remember either, do you? What it was like before you came here."

"...Yeah. I don't remember."

"Neither do I. Not even my family or friends. I don't remember them at all."

"Yep," she said.

"So, on that note," he said nervously, "could it be... Like, for me, I joined a party, and I think I met them all for the first time here, but maybe that's not the case, right?"

"...You might have known each other from before?" she asked.

"Well, I'm just saying that it's a possibility."

"It could be. For instance, with me and..."

Choco looked at Haruhiro. Just a brief glance. She immediately looked away again.

"...You, too," she finished.

Haruhiro took a deep breath. "...We could've, right? That's a possibility."

"But..." she began.

"Yeah?"

"...Since we don't remember it, it doesn't matter."

"That's not..."

...True, he wanted to say.

But, it was just like she said.

No matter what had been between them in the past—whether they'd been friends, lovers, or family—if they both didn't remember it, it didn't mean anything.

It didn't mean anything.

"Come to think of it, I haven't asked your name yet," Choco asked.

"My name?" Haruhiro felt like he'd been sucker-punched.

Choco didn't know Haruhiro's name.

"Ah... Yeah, that's right, isn't it?" he asked.

Of course.

They'd only just met, so there's no way she'd have known it.

It really was just a coincidence. Before he'd come to Grimgar, Haruhiro had known a girl named Choco. This girl here now just happened to be called Choco, too.

"You weak-willed wussy." It sounds like I've heard it before—but that's just what it feels like.

In the end, that was all there was to it, nothing more.

"I'm Haruhiro," he said.

"Haruhiro..." Choco lowered her eyes, then glanced at Haruhiro again. "...Hmm. Well, can I call you Hiro?"

"Sure."

It was really weird. Why were his eyes getting all hot? Haruhiro didn't understand it.

Yume called Haruhiro Haru-kun. For Merry, he was Haru. That was generally how it went.

But, somehow... I've been called that before—that's what it feels like. Called Hiro.

By someone, somewhere.

"I'm okay with that," he said. "Of course."

"I see." Choco crouched down, peering at Haruhiro's face. "...Are you okay?"

"Huh? What do you mean?" Haruhiro rubbed his eyes with one finger. "I'm fine, you know?"

Choco seemed suspicious.

Haruhiro stood up, stretching a little. "Better hit the hay... What are you up to, Choco? It's pretty late."

"A walk, outside," she said.

"Can't sleep?"

"Yeah. It happens, sometimes."

Well, we may run into one another occasionally, then, he thought.

Who cares about some past I don't even remember properly? There's still the future to come.

Right now, the Choco in front of me seems kind of gloomy, unsociable, and hard to approach. Her big eyes remind me of a little animal, full of caution, and she doesn't look people in the eye when she speaks to them. But, when she occasionally stares at me, it makes my heart race.

She's probably the kind of girl I like. At the very least, I'm interested in her. What's wrong with that?

"Choco, you're a thief?" he asked.

"...How could you tell?" she asked.

"I can tell by your equipment, and such. I'm a thief, too, after all."

"Ah. You look like one," she agreed.

"Huh? What part of me?"

"You're lanky."

"No, that may be true, but...I'm a thief because I'm lanky? Is that the image you have? Is that what thieves are like to you? Why did you become a thief?"

"I just sort of did."

"Going with the flow?" he asked.

"Something like that."

"What's your trade name?" Haruhiro asked her.

"The one we only use with other thieves?"

"Yeah. Since we're both thieves, and all."

"...I kind of don't want to say," Choco said.

"No, well, I'm not that fond of mine, either..."

"It's something someone else gave me, anyway," she added.

"Well then, how about we both say them at the same time?"

"The same time?"

"We'll do it with a one, two, three, go."

"Okay," she said.

"All right. One, two, three—go!"

"Cheeky Cat."

"Old Cat."

They looked at one another.

Choco let out a little burst of laughter.

"Wh-what? What is it?" Haruhiro stammered.

"I mean, come on, 'Old Cat'?"

"...Yeah, I know. I get told I have sleepy eyes all the time. I must look like an old man, I'm sure."

"I probably got mine because of my eyes, too," Choco said.

"Because they look cheeky? Not because you act that way, too?"

"Could be."

"And wait, we're both cats," he added.

"That's some coincidence," she said.

"It really is..."

Is it just a coincidence?

Of course, it probably is.

"Is your mentor Barbara-sensei?" he asked.

"Who's Barbara?" she responded.

"Oh, she isn't. Well, she's there. There's a person at the thieves' guild called Barbara."

"Hmm," Choco said.

"Is your mentor a man?" he asked.

"Yeah. He's scary."

"Barbara-sensei, too," he agreed. "She's a woman, but she's insanely scary..."

"I should never have become a thief," Choco said.

"I hear it's hard at the other places, too, though," Haruhiro told her.

"There are thorns on every path?" she asked.

"I'd say so."

"I want to take it easy," she complained.

"Well, yeah, if I could take it easy, I think that would be for the best, too..."

"Do you find it all a pain?" she asked.

"Yeah," he agreed. "I'm always quick to think that. 'Ahh, this is such a pain.'"

"Same here."

"I see."

"Hey," Choco said.

"Huh?" he asked.

"Hiro, is your party accepting the order, too?"

"The order..."

This time, he'd really been caught by surprise. For a moment, he honestly thought he'd been punched in the chest with something not all that hard.

"The order... Wait, 'too'? Choco, your party's participating? In that operation...?"

"I don't want to do it, though. It seems kind of dangerous." When Choco let out a heavy breath, her bangs shook slightly. "But, apparently, we are."

Grimgar
of
Fantasy and Ash

6. The Vote

"Okay, we'll put it to a vote, then."

One night had ended...and now it was night again.

Having made a tidy profit on their volunteer soldier work for the day and retired to a corner of Sherry's Tavern, as usual, Haruhiro and the party were planning again today.

They'd ordered drinks, which were already laid out on the table, but nobody had touched them.

Haruhiro looked at each of his comrades' faces.

Ranta had his arms crossed, looking all smug and self-important.

Moguzo must've been rather tense, because he had a stern look on his face.

Shihoru was looking downwards.

Yume looked like she was praying that this would end soon.

Merry looked like she was keeping her calm.

Haruhiro sighed deeply. "The subject is whether or not we participate in the order for Operation 'Two-Headed Snake.' All in favor, raise your hands."

"Yeah!" Ranta immediately raised both of his hands.

Moguzo followed.

Yume kept her hand at table-level, raising it a little, then lowering it again.

Merry remained stiff and unmoving.

When Haruhiro gently raised his hand, Shihoru raised her own, as if being dragged along.

"...Huh," she said, looking back and forth from her own hand to Haruhiro's.

"...Hoh," Yume let out an odd sound in surprise.

Merry's eyes went wide, "...Huh?"

Moguzo blinked repeatedly, tilting his head to the side, "Hm?"

"Wha—" Ranta jumped out of his chair, his eyes darting around as he counted the number of hands. "One, two, three, four, five... Five?!"

"No, Ranta, you just counted both of your hands," Haruhiro said.

"Huhh?! I did not! Like I'd do that! No, wait, maybe I did. Yeah, I did. So, what then, it's four? Four. That's a majority, huh."

"Yeah, it kind of is," Haruhiro said. "So, that settles it. We'll accept the order."

"R-right," said Ranta, looking uncertain.

"What?" Haruhiro asked. "That's what we voted. There shouldn't be a problem."

"I don't have a problem with it—but, wait! Haruhiro! You're in favor?! What's brought this up?!" Ranta exclaimed.

"Not 'up.' You mean 'on,' right?"

"Shut up! You're such a pain! It doesn't matter, really! You're a coward to the core, so if you're voting in favor, what are you plotting— No, don't tell me! I've got it! I've got you figured out! I'll bet it was

clear that you'd lose the vote even if you voted against, so you figured it'd rock the boat less if you voted in favor, or something lame like that! Bullseye, right?! That's so like you!" Ranta slapped Haruhiro repeatedly on the shoulder.

That hurts, you know, when you slap me like that, Haruhiro thought. *Hold back a little, will you? You're making me mad. Why do you have to be so ill-mannered? Is it because you're Ranta?*

"...Don't just decide that," Haruhiro said, brushing Ranta's hand away. "That's not what I'm thinking at all. Besides, if I hadn't approved, we wouldn't have had a majority."

"Don't be so picky about every little thing," Ranta scoffed. "What are you, a magnifying glass?"

"Magnifying glasses don't speak."

"See, that's called being picky."

"You're too imprecise."

"I don't sweat the small stuff, so call me magnanimous!" Ranta exclaimed. "It means kingly! Because I'm fit to be a king!"

"No, it doesn't quite mean that," Merry coldly corrected him.

With an "Urkh..." Ranta fell silent, though only momentarily. He recovered in no time. "Well, what, then?! Haruhiro! What did you vote in favor for?! Spill your guts! Come on, puke!"

Yume grimaced. "That's filthy..."

"...Yeah... His very existence is..." Shihoru said, looking at Ranta as if he were something unclean.

Hold on, 'His very existence is...'? Haruhiro thought. *Little harsh there, Shihoru. Well, Ranta doesn't seem to care, so it's fine, I guess. Still, it's impressive he can just take that. If she said that to me, it'd get me down, and I probably wouldn't recover for a while.*

"I'd like to know..." Moguzo took a sip of his beer. "I'd like to know your reason for it, too...maybe? I thought you were opposing it because you were concerned for all of us. You know...since you're our leader."

"He's garbage at it, though!" Ranta knocked back his beer, then guffawed heartily.

"That's not true," Moguzo protested. "Haruhiro-kun is trying his hardest for us!"

"Yeah, yeah! Moguzo's right! Haru-kun's doin' a great job!" Yume added.

"...I think so, too," Shihoru put in.

"Agreed," Merry finished.

"What's this?" Ranta shouted. "Ganging up on me?! Well, I don't care, it doesn't matter to me one bit! Bring it on!"

Haruhiro covered his mouth with his hand. *Oh, man. Oh, man. I must have the dumbest grin on my face right now. Somehow, they have a higher opinion of my work than I expected...? Well, Ranta's opinion was a bit off. Then again, Ranta himself is a bit off.*

But this isn't the time to feel all giddy about it.

Haruhiro coughed politely. "There were various reasons..."

Like being worried about Choco.

He didn't know much about Choco's party, but he was sure they weren't hyper-competent rookies like Team Renji. If they were, the other volunteer soldiers would've talked, and Haruhiro would have heard about it.

Haruhiro's party wasn't particularly strong, but if an even more inexperienced group was planning to join an operation to attack an orcish keep, that was just reckless. It was clearly way too dangerous.

That said, even if they joined the operation as well, that wouldn't mean he could protect Choco. After all, they weren't in the same party. But if he were close by when something happened, he might be able to help a little.

I can't say that, though.

I can't tell my comrades that, of course.

Besides, Choco being there was just an added bonus.

More than anything, Haruhiro had decided they should accept the order for their own sakes.

"First, there's the reward," he said. "The fact that we'll be getting one gold between the advance payment and the rest of the payment is a big deal. If it's not wrapped up in a day, from the second day on, we'll be given a stipend of thirty silver a day. Also, there may be special compensation awarded in the field, too, right, Ranta?"

"Yeah," Ranta said, shrugging his shoulders. He was probably trying to look cool, but he didn't. "If we take down strong enemies, like their commanders, I guess. Sounds like there's a lot of stuff like that."

"Well, I don't think we need to actively aim for them if it would mean pushing ourselves," Haruhiro said, slapping his hands down on the table. "...That's the point."

"Hmm?" Yume asked, screwing up her face and tilting her head to the side. "What's the point?"

"You know, for this order, we get paid just for participating in it, right?" Haruhiro asked. "Even if we can't accomplish—or don't accomplish—anything, we'll receive the fixed payment. If things look bad, we don't have to do anything crazy."

"You gutless coward!" Ranta flipped him the bird and stuck his tongue out. "You loser!"

"Call me whatever you want. I don't care in the slightest."

"Haruhiro, you weakling!" Ranta shouted.

"Yeah, yeah."

"You piece of shit!"

"...Come on, man."

"You're small, too!" Ranta added.

"That's got nothing to do with this!"

"Small...?" Yume asked, puffing up one of her cheeks and tilting her head to the side.

"...Y-Yume, he means..." Shihoru began.

What was Shihoru trying to explain to her in a whisper? Haruhiro couldn't say he wasn't curious.

"Anyway," Haruhiro said, scratching his head.

He'd agonized a lot before coming to this decision. Finding out Choco's party would be participating in the operation had just given him an excuse. It had only been that, an excuse; it hadn't been the deciding factor. This was the decision he'd come to after all that agonizing.

"Rather than try to pull off some glorious display of heroics, it's better if we all make it out of this safely," Haruhiro said. "That's what I think. But our line of work isn't so easy that we'll be able to get through it without taking any risks whatsoever. If we want to live longer in this harsh environment, we have to get stronger. We need to build up more experience. They say you're not a real volunteer soldier until you've killed an orc. So there's going to come a time when we have to challenge ourselves to face orcs. In that case, why not do it now? During this operation, we'll have other volunteer soldiers with us, so it's not a bad situation to do it in, right?"

Shihoru gulped.

Yume said "Ooh," her eyes widening with excitement.

Moguzo looked intently at Haruhiro while Merry listened quietly.

Heh heh heh, heh heh heh..." Ranta suddenly put on a villainous smile. "Wa ha ha ha ha! Gwahahahaha! Haruhirooo! You really *are* a hooooooooopelessly, seriously, pitifully pathetic chicken, huh?! Aren't you embarrassed to even be alive? Hmmmm?"

"...Right back at you. I'm amazed you can live with yourself with that awful personality of yours."

"Awful personalityyyyyy? Huhhhhhhhhh? What are you talking abouuuuuuut? I just tell it like it is, you knoooooooow?"

If I see that line the next time I'm behind Ranta, I'll backstab him without hesitation.

Well, for now, I have to hold back. Yeah. Okay. Patience, patience, patience, patience. If I give him the time of day, he'll just get worse. Ignore him.

"Besides," Haruhiro said aloud, "say what you will about us, we're the party that took down Death Spots. And the keep this time is called Deadhead. The names are close. I dunno, don't you think it's a sign? It could be."

"Wow!" Moguzo's huge body bent backwards. He must've been surprised, but he ended up surprising Haruhiro, too. "N-now that you mention it, you're right! Death Spots and Deadhead... I never noticed...!"

Yume looked excited. "Whoo. Yume, too. Yume, too. That's right. Death Spots and Deck Rot, they're real similar. But Death Spots sounds like 'date spot,' too, huh?"

"...Not Deck Rot, Deadhead, okay?" Haruhiro corrected her, as if out of some sense of duty. "'Death Spots' and 'date spot' are kind of close, though... Anyway, are you against it after all, Yume?"

"Hmmmeow," Yume said. "If everyone says they're gonna do it, y'know, Yume's gonna think it's okay to try it, too."

"How about you, Merry?" Haruhiro asked.

Merry nodded with something resembling a smile. "If that's what everyone's decided, I'm okay with it. I'll just do everything I can to keep you all alive."

"M-me, too!" Moguzo thumped his chest. "My role's different from Merry's, but if I do my job right, it helps to protect everyone! I'll do it! I'll work hard!"

"Well, then," Ranta grinned. "It's unanimous. Everyone's hugely in favor, right?"

Ranta, the man with a smile that pisses people off. Oh, how I envy that gift of his.

No, not really.

Like I ever would.

Haruhiro lifted his porcelain mug full of mead. "Let's go with that."

Grimgar
of
Fantasy and Ash

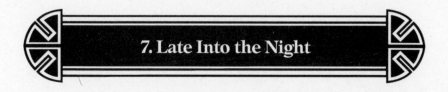

7. Late Into the Night

Once the decision was made, the time flew by.

They went to the Volunteer Soldier Corps office to accept the order, went about their work as normal, waited nervously for the moment to come, and then all of a sudden, the operation was tomorrow.

They were to gather first thing tomorrow morning—though, actually, because the assault on Deadhead Watching Keep and Riverside Iron Fortress began at dawn, they had to be by the north gate of Alterna at three o'clock in the morning.

The bells in Alterna only rang from six in the morning to six at night in two hour intervals, and Haruhiro and the others didn't own a clock. They'd seen them for sale, but apparently only dwarven craftsmen could make them, or something like that, so the price was high enough to make their eyes bulge out. Fortunately, there was a wall clock in the front hall of the volunteer soldier lodging house, so they could check the time there.

They aimed to rise from their beds at two o'clock—or thereabouts. Well, if even one of them woke up around then, they just had to go around rousing everyone else, so it'd work out somehow.

In preparation for tomorrow, Haruhiro and the others went to sleep around sunset. More precisely, that was when they lay down to bed and started trying to get some sleep.

"This is impossible!"

In the darkened room, Ranta was the first to start squirming, of course, but this time Haruhiro felt the same way.

"You can't just suddenly expect us to fall asleep at this time of day..." Ranta griped.

"Y-yeah..." Apparently Moguzo agreed. "I can never get enough sleep, but I'm not tired yet..."

"If we can't sleep anyway, you wanna go?!" Ranta shouted. "Launch a little raid?!"

"What do you mean 'a raid'...? Hold on, Ranta, we're already having enough trouble trying to get to sleep, so pipe down a little, would you?" Haruhiro complained.

"U-um, Ranta-kun, go where?" Moguzo stuttered.

"Huh?! Buddy, I mean the girls' room, of course!"

"Huh...?" Moguzo asked.

"There's no way we're going..." Haruhiro said with a sigh. "Besides, what would you go there for?"

"What would I go there for?" Ranta demanded. "There's only one thing."

"One thing?"

"The one thing is...that one thing!"

"Again, what thing?" Haruhiro asked.

"Ah—"

"Ah?"

"Uh."

"Uh?"

"Boo..."

"Boo? What?"

"...What starts with 'boo'?" Ranta asked.

"Don't ask me," Haruhiro said. "You're the one who started this. Are you just making it up as you go along? If you haven't thought of something, why not just say so?"

"I have been thinking! I've been thinking like crazy! Boo...B-Boo... Moguzo! Boo!"

"M-me?" Moguzo stammered. "Boo...? Bo...Boo...Boooo...."

"Keep it up, Moguzo! It's coming out! You're almost there! Go on!"

"...Bootlicking?"

"You dolt! Moguzo, you moron! What kind of guy charges into the girls' room, then asks them to lick boots with him?! Are you some king of pervert?! If it starts with 'boo,' I can only mean one thing! Boobs, duh!"

"...Uwah."

"What, Haruhiro? What's the 'uwah' for? You like boobs, too! Because you're a dude! If you call yourself a man, all of us love boobs!"

"Don't just *decide* that..." Haruhiro muttered.

"Oh, ho! Well, do you hate them, then? If there were a pair of boobs in front of you right now, you wouldn't feel anything? I'm talking a nice, hefty pair of knockers here, you know?"

"...Well, it's not like I wouldn't feel *anything*."

"Moguzo, you like 'em too, right?" Ranta demanded. "Boobs."

"Huh...? W-well... Sure, as much as the next guy..."

"Stop it, Moguzo," Haruhiro said. "You don't have to engage with him."

"See! You both like them, too! Gwahaha! In the end, you're male, too! Now, let's go, come on!"

"Seriously, what are you going to do there?" Haruhiro demanded.

"I'm gonna squeeze them, that's what!" Ranta declared. "I'll squeeze them! I'll squeeze them like crazy!"

"...That's practically rape, man."

"I'm not gonna go that far!" Ranta snapped. "I'm just gonna squeeze them! I'll just squeeze their boobs, that's all! That ought to be fine! It's all okay!"

"No, that's not okay to do, as a person..."

"Well, yeah," Ranta agreed suddenly.

"Right?" Haruhiro said.

"Besides, it'd be awkward, y'know," Ranta added. "Even if I forced them to let me squeeze them, it'd be pointless, wouldn't it? What then? I want a 'You can squeeze them.' Or rather, a 'Please, squeeze them.' It's gotta be something like that. You've gotta have love."

"What's this, all of a sudden?" Haruhiro asked. "You're creeping me out."

"You moron, this is the time for talking about love, obviously!" Ranta shouted. "You know what's up, right? Yume and Shihoru'll be doing it too. No doubt about it. They're doing it. They're doing it like crazy. I mean, they're girls, after all."

"Yeah..." Moguzo grunted in agreement.

Haruhiro turned over in bed. "...Is that how it is?"

"Damn straight it is," Ranta said firmly. "Girls and talking about love are inseparable. They're as closely connected as old men and fires.

Yeah...forget that comparison. It failed. But these creatures called girls, their heads are seriously, seriously filled with nothing but love. They're talking about it now. 'Shihoru, Shihoru, who do you like? Whaa? What about you, Yume?' Like that. They are *so* doing it."

"No...I'll bet they aren't talking about anything like that."

"Haruhiro, you don't get girls at all," Ranta said scornfully. "They're these bizarre little creatures who'd sooner fall in love than eat. When they fall down, they don't just get up. They fall in love. If they fall down seven times, they'll fall in love eight. That's what girls are like. So? How about you?"

"Huh? How about what?" Haruhiro asked.

"Who do you like?"

"Huh...?"

Perhaps it was because he was completely unprepared for the question. Bam, bam... Two faces appeared in his vision. The order they appeared in was... Haruhiro wasn't sure, himself. The two faces seemed to flicker back and forth.

"...What do you mean, who?" he asked.

"Want me to take a guess? It's Yume, yeah?"

"Wha—"

"Bullseye, huh? Merry's got the best looks, no question there, but she's *clearly* out of your league. Shihoru's got huge boobs, which is a big point in her favor. Her face is decently cute, too. But that personality of hers seems like a pain, and she doesn't talk to guys much, anyway. An indecisive guy with low self-esteem like you is gonna go for an airhead like Yume. That's just how it is."

"...Well, sorry for being indecisive," Haruhiro snapped.

"It's not okay. It's annoying. Girls don't go for that, man," Ranta said. "To be blunt."

"I'm pretty sure girls aren't into you, either, for an entirely different reason."

Also, you weren't even right. Haruhiro almost said it, but he was under no obligation to correct Ranta. *That's not how it is. I don't have any feelings of love. At least, it hasn't gone that far yet—I think. Probably.*

"Ha!" Ranta declared. "You're the kind of moron who can't tell that I ooze charm. That's why girls aren't into you. Haruhiro, that's enough out of you. Moguzo, what about you? Who do you like?"

"I-it's not that there's anyone I like, or anything..."

"Nuh-uh, there's gotta be someone," Ranta said confidently. "If there are men and there are women, there's no way you don't have someone! Our male instincts naturally select a female."

"It sounds so raw...when you put it like that..." Moguzo murmured.

"That's because we're alive. We're young, too! If we aren't raw and full of life, what are we? Let's cut to the chase! Moguzo, who do you want to breed with?!"

"Ranta..." Haruhiro said with exasperation.

"Huh? What, Haruhiro? I'm just putting it plainly. Because when a man is looking for a woman, that's basically what it's about."

"B-but, Ranta-kun," Moguzo stammered. "I don't think like that... you know?"

"Well, what do you think like? Come on, say it. Talk."

"It's more like...I *admire* her, you could say," Moguzo said.

"Oh, ho?"

"Or I sometimes think, 'She's so pretty...'"

"So, Moguzo, you're gunning for Merry, then!"

"Whaa?! H-how did you know?! I-I'm not gunning for her,

though..."

"Of course I'd know," Ranta smirked. "If you say pretty, Merry's the only one of them that fits."

Haruhiro shook his head. "...You only ever say things you shouldn't."

"Wroooong," Ranta retorted. "I'm a man who only speaks the truuuuth. No matter how you look at Yume or Shihoru, neither of them is what you'd call a real beauty. Dig the wax out of those sleepy eyes of yours and take a proper look, dammit."

"You don't dig wax out of your eyes, that'd go terribly, and how many times do I have to tell you not to talk about my eyes?" Haruhiro asked.

"Still, though," Ranta mused. "Moguzo wants Merry, huh. Nice choice. Yep, that's my partner for you."

Moguzo laughed nervously. "Ha... hahaha... Um, but, I just think she's pretty, that's all..."

"Still, man, Merry said it herself," Ranta added. "If she had to choose one of us, it'd be Moguzo, or something like that."

"...Y-yeah," Moguzo agreed. "The truth is, after that... I don't know, but just a little...I've been more—conscious?—of her..."

"Conscious..." Haruhiro mumbled. Moguzo had quietly been developing an interest in the opposite sex, weird as it was to put it that way. Still, it was kind of a shock.

"Gwahahaha!" Ranta was strangely excited for some reason. "Moguzo, you dog, you! Push, push, and push harder! Who knows, maybe it'll even work out for you?!"

"Ah, no, I-I couldn't..."

"Moguzo, buddy, let me tell you something, since I'm your partner.

Life may seem long, but it's short. You've gotta do what you've gotta do, you know? So that you have no regrets, okay? So confess your love!"

"Mrgh! I can't do that..."

"Just confess, okay?!" Ranta ordered. "Do it tomorrow!"

"I'm telling you, I can't..."

"You can't because you *think* you can't! If you think you can do it, you can! That's how it works! Right, Haruhiro? I'm right, aren't I?"

"Huh? Ah, um, yeah, well, I suppose—Hey, wait, don't suddenly drag me into this!"

"You idiot, aren't you going to support Moguzo?" Ranta retorted. "We're comrades, aren't we?"

"Support him...?" Haruhiro muttered. "Well, it's not like I don't, but..."

"Don't you want him to find happiness?!"

"I do..."

"Then he should confess! He oughta confess! He's got to show off his love confession dance!"

"What the hell is a 'love confession dance' supposed to be?" Haruhiro demanded.

"It's a traditional performance you put on while confessing your love! That kind of stuff exists! I just decided it does! Okay, dance for us, Moguzo! Do the I Love You dance!"

Moguzo didn't move. "...I'm not going to dance...okay?"

"Yeah, that figures," Ranta said. "It'd be awkward for me if you did, anyway. I was just saying it! I'm first-rate at just saying stuff!"

"Ranta, you're totally third-rate," Haruhiro retorted.

"If a fifth-rate guy like you says that, Haruhiro, I don't even care."

"And who do you like, anyway?" Haruhiro demanded. "You asked me and Moguzo, but you haven't said anything for yourself."

"Y-yeah, that's right," Moguzo agreed. "Ranta-kun, you tell us, too."

"Huhh? Meeee? You want meeee to? What, guys, do you reeeeally want to know?"

"If you're asking whether I actually want to know, I'm really iffy on that..." Haruhiro said.

"I-I think I want to know, maybe," Moguzo mumbled.

"You want to know thaaaat badly?"

"...Honestly, I don't care that much," said Haruhiro.

"I want to know...okay?" Moguzo said. "Pretty badly."

"You're hopeless, you know that. Well, if you insist..."

Haruhiro sensed Ranta turning over in bed. He sure was making a big deal out of this. No matter how you looked at it, wasn't he making way too big of a deal out of this?

But then, after all of that, what did he do?

"I'm not goooonna tell you, mooooorons."

"Man, don't screw with us...!" Haruhiro shouted.

"Y-you're awful, Ranta-kun!"

"Gwaaaahahahahahahaha! Don't think you'll get a secret out of me so easily! I got your secrets perfectly, though!"

"Tell us! You're being cowardly!" Haruhiro snapped.

"Y-yeah! It's not fair if you're the only one who doesn't say!"

"If you don't like it, then make me talk!" Ranta shouted. "You! Can't! Do! It!"

"I swear, I'll make you talk!" Haruhiro snarled.

"I'll twist your arm if I have to..." Moguzo murmured.

"Hey! Hold on, Moguzo, hey! No, brute strength is—Gwargh...!"

Grimgar of Fantasy and Ash

8. Meat Shield

Beneath the still dark sky, there was a raucous gathering in front of Alterna's north gate.

The "Blue Snake Force" which would set out to take Deadhead Watching Keep was to be led by Wren Water, a Brigadier General in the Alterna Frontier Army. At his command were 500 warriors, 100 paladins, and 100 hunters, as well as a number of priests, bringing the total to a little over 700 for the main force. They were accompanied by a detached force consisting of thirty-seven volunteer soldier parties, for a total of 197 participants. These were to be led by the chief of the Volunteer Soldier Corps Red Moon Office, as well as its host, Britney, or Bri-chan, as he preferred to be called.

In addition, there were the well-wishers and rubberneckers, as well as merchants not about to miss a chance to sell their wares, so there were more than 1,000 people gathered in the area. "Noisy" didn't even begin to describe how loud it was.

Incidentally, the "Red Snake Force" setting out for Riverside Iron Fortress was composed of 1,000 warriors, 300 paladins, 200 dread knights, 300 cavalry, and 50 priests, all from the Frontier Army, led by General Graham Rasentra, for an incredible total of 1,850 troops in the main force. There was also a commando unit centered around Soma's Day Breakers that was composed of 55 parties, a total of over 300 people, so it was even more incredible.

Furthermore, the defense of Alterna would be carried out by the remaining soldiers of the Frontier Army under the command of Brigadier General Ian Ratty.

Haruhiro didn't know much about General Graham Rasentra or Brigadier General Ian Ratty, or rather, he hadn't even heard their names before.

Brigadier General Wren Water was way up at the front, right next to the north gate. He looked neat and trim in his shining white armor, and had a look that was, to use a somewhat old-sounding expression, ruggedly handsome. He didn't seem like a bad guy, but he was cold towards the volunteer soldiers somehow, as if he had a lot of pride. His armor bore the hexagram sign of the god of light, Lumiaris, so he was likely a paladin.

The internal ranking of the Blue Snake Force was apparent at a glance, with the paladins and priests around Wren Water, the warriors behind them, and the hunters behind the warriors. The detached force was even further back.

The main force was standing in relatively orderly rows, with superior officers yelling at anyone who stepped out of line, but the volunteer soldiers in the detached force were a real mess. They were divided into parties, for the most part, but they did as they pleased, standing and chatting, sitting around, or wandering here and there.

Is this really okay? Haruhiro thought, unsure, but it didn't seem like it was particularly going to be a problem.

Actually, the detached force were probably being left to their own devices. Surely, the main force must have looked at them and thought, *Do what you want, as if we care. We in the regular forces aren't like you volunteer soldiers,* or something like that.

He didn't know anyone in the Frontier Army, but Haruhiro had lived here in Alterna long enough to have a vague sense that that was the case. Volunteer soldiers were outsiders to begin with, so the regular soldiers saw them as untrustworthy, somehow. The volunteer soldiers didn't particularly like them, either.

However, for someone who'd achieved as much as Soma, and who was held in such high esteem, it was a different matter.

All of the famous volunteer soldiers like him were participating in the Red Snake Force's commando unit, so the Blue Snake Force's detached force were thought of as the dregs. And ranked even beneath those dregs were—let it be no secret—Haruhiro and his party.

That said, even in the detached force, there were powerful volunteer soldiers who they respected, or who they were forced to respect. The ones who stood out most were the Wild Angels, led by Kajiko.

The Wild Angels were, without exception, women, and all of them wore white feathered stoles, along with helmets, hats, bandannas, or hairbands decorated with the same white feathers.

Not only were the members all women, they didn't let any men get close to them. If a man tried to approach, they'd shout loudly to intimidate him into backing off.

They were super scary.

In particular, when it came to Kajiko, who was tall, terrifyingly beautiful, and carried a long, katana-like sword, her eyes were seriously crazy. If Kajiko ever glared at him, Haruhiro was confident that that alone would be enough to nearly kill him.

Still, there was another group that was just as intimidating as the Wild Angels, a group that'd enlisted at the same time as them.

Team Renji.

Just by standing there, Renji was so imposing that it felt like a low rumbling sound effect might start to play. He seemed so blindingly brilliant that Haruhiro couldn't bear to look directly at him.

Renji had the sword once carried by the orc Ish Dogran slung over his back. As for the sword Renji had used before, it'd been given to Ron, who was sitting on his haunches next to him. Renji was self-possessed and looking around contemptuously at his surroundings, but Ron was blatantly staring people down. Even if he was a small-time goon compared to Renji, there weren't many who could remain calm and composed when faced with Ron's gaze, given his buzzcut and violent appearance.

Sassa, who was standing behind Renji, had a mature aura about her—or rather an incredibly adult sexiness—and Adachi with his thick black-rimmed glasses looked like a world-shaking genius.

Beside Renji—or rather, within arm's reach of him—even Chibi, who was standing there small and adorable, started to look like a mascot with some unknown and threatening power hidden within her, so Renji seriously had an incredible presence.

Even Kajiko herself seemed to have taken note of Renji. She'd been staring at him hard for a while now. Whether Renji noticed or not, he was completely ignoring her.

I just hope it doesn't spark any conflict later, Haruhiro thought.

Guess that's not any of my business, huh? Yeah, it's definitely not.

For Haruhiro, both the Wild Angels and Team Renji were so far above him as to be out of reach. Each person had their own station in life. They had their business; he had his.

Haruhiro's eyes met Choco's. He greeted her with his eyes, and she gave him a little nod in return.

Behind the main force, in the very, very back of the detached force, that was where Haruhiro and the others had taken up their positions. If you went by their experience and ability, well, it was a suitable spot for them.

Choco's party was a little bit ahead of Haruhiro's.

How am I supposed to feel about that? Nah, it's fine, really.

From what Haruhiro could tell, the pleasant warrior who had a face that probably made him popular with girls seemed to be the leader of Choco's party. They'd formed into a ring around Mr. Pleasant, who was chatting away merrily, so there was little doubt about it.

There was also the girl with the short hair who'd been with Choco when he first met her. Ms. Short Hair was a mage.

Other than that, there was a man in priest's clothes and a couple guys in what looked like warrior equipment. One of the warriors was pretty tall, but Mr. Tall seemed moody, like he'd be hard to get close to. The other warrior was always laughing like an idiot. Laughing Man also seemed to be making a lot of passes at Choco.

Choco looks kind of bothered by it. Cut that out, man. You're pissing me off.

Not that me being pissed off means anything. They're comrades in the same party, while I've only talked to her a bit, after all.

"...Hahh. Hahh. Hahh..." Moguzo's breathing was weirdly rough.

Was he excited? He was probably feeling tense, like you might expect. He kept taking his helmet off and putting it back on at high speed.

Haruhiro slapped Moguzo on the back as hard as he could.

"Moguzo!"

"Ow?!"

"What's up?" he asked. "Feeling tense?"

"Huh? Ah, y-yeah... Just a little. No, a lot..."

"Well, I can't blame you there," Haruhiro said. "We've never been in an atmosphere like this before, after all."

"B-but, Haruhiro-kun, you're not that tense...are you?" Moguzo asked nervously.

"Do I not look it? Well, that's...not entirely untrue."

True enough, Haruhiro wasn't feeling very tense. In fact, he wasn't feeling tense at all. He was calm. Though, in the end, it had taken him a long time to get to sleep, so he was a bit tired.

Yume let out an odd little laugh. "Haru-kun's always unsweatin', y'know."

"U-unsweatin'...?" Haruhiro repeated uncertainly.

"E-erm..." Shihoru quickly stepped in to explain. "I think she means he doesn't sweat the small stuff, and tries to be magnanimous, maybe..."

Yume cocked her head to the side. "Magnanimous?"

"Let me say right now," Haruhiro added, just to be sure, "'magnanimous' doesn't mean 'kingly,' okay? It's read *ouyou*, but it can't be written with the kanji for king-like. That wouldn't even be a proper word..."

"*Ouyou*...?" Yume thought for a moment, then turned her palm towards him. "Oh!"

"O-oh?" Haruhiro went along with it and clapped his hand against Yume's.

Then, Yume held out the opposite hand. "Yo!"

"...Yo?" Haruhiro pressed his hand against Yume's and it ended up with them having both hands pressed together.

What is this?

Yume held both of Haruhiro's hands tight. "Oh! Yo!"

"...Yeah. Yeah...?"

"This's it, y'know," Yume said. "It's what comes to mind when you say *ouyou*."

"Th-this...does?"

"Hrm. Yume's not sure of herself, but it's kinda like this?"

"Kinda, huh..." Haruhiro kind of glanced in Choco's direction.

By coincidence—yes, he was sure it was coincidence—Choco was looking in his direction. She quickly looked down, though. It felt kind of awkward.

"...Um, Yume," Haruhiro said. "Can we let go now?"

"Ho? Sure. Guess so. Ah, Haru-kun, Haru-kun!"

"Huh? What?" he asked.

"Just now, Yume was thinkin', Haru-kun's hands, they sure are warm. Why's that?" she asked.

"Dunno..."

Haruhiro tried touching his left hand with his right. Were they really warm? They felt normal to him. Though, maybe it wasn't something you'd notice yourself.

Moguzo was still taking his helmet off and putting it back on. It didn't look like his nervousness would be cured so easily. Even so, Haruhiro couldn't just leave him be. He was about to call out to Moguzo again when Merry beat him to it.

"Moguzo-kun."

"Yesh?"

Wait, what's yesh supposed to be? What's a yesh?

Moguzo had a look on his face like he'd just run into a deep-sea fish on land.

Merry put a hand on his shoulder. "Take a deep breath."

"A d-d-deep breath... *Uh... Hooooooooooooo...Hahhhhhhhhhhhhhhhhh-hhhhhhhhhh.* Urkh, i-it hurts..."

"Gently," she said. "Calm down."

"Y-yeah. Hoooooooooooooooo. Hahhhhhhhhhhhhhhhhhh."

"One more time."

"Hoooooooo. Hahhhhhhhhhh... Ah! Th-that calmed me down a bit...maybe."

"Normally, breathing is something you do unconsciously," Merry said. "Because of that, if you focus on breathing, you can gain control of your feelings, and of other things as well. That's what I do when I can't calm down."

"Th-thank you, Merry-san. I'd gotten really rattled, and—"

"You know, probably..." Haruhiro began.

Would it be best not to interject? Haruhiro hesitated a bit, but it was a good opportunity, so he wanted to say this. Honestly, it was something that'd been nagging at him all along, and he was concerned about it.

"We're relying on you pretty heavily, aren't we, Moguzo?" he asked. "I think that's got to put a lot of pressure on you, doesn't it?"

"...Huh? Ah, no, n-not really..."

"But, to be honest, I think we're going to keep relying on you from here out," Haruhiro said. "You're a warrior, and the party's tank, so that's part of it, of course, but that's not all, you know. Moguzo, you're seriously reliable. That's why I want you to build up more and more confidence. I mean, if we think about whose growth is most apparent in our group, who's leveled up the most, that'd have to be you, Moguzo. I'm sure everyone feels the same."

"You dolt!" Ranta jumped up like a monkey. "If anyone's leveled up to the max, it's me, duh! If I've leveled up thirty times, Moguzo's leveled up, like, twenty-five, maybe!"

"That's awfully humble, coming from you," Haruhiro said.

"Whaaaat?! I-is it...? Then, well, it's fifty level-ups for me, and around twenty-five for Moguzo!"

"What, you're not lowering Moguzo's number, just raising yours...?"

"Well, duh!" Ranta shot back. "I'm the man who'll rule the world, you know?!"

"...The people all around us are laughing at you," Shihoru said with a cold sneer on her face.

"Whaaaat?!" Ranta cried. "That's cruel! You're serious!"

"Yume, yeah, she thinks Moguzo's real amazin'," Yume agreed. "We wouldn't get nowhere without Moguzo. He's our meat shield!"

"Meat shield..." Merry's face twitched a little.

"Fwah? Is it no good callin' him a meat shield? Yume meant it as a compliment, though."

"No, um, actually..." Moguzo shook his head, then nodded. "I'm happy about it. I don't know how to say it, but if I can be everyone's meat shield, I want to be."

"Yeah!" Ranta put an arm around Moguzo's shoulder. "I'm

counting on you, partner! No, meat shield!"

"I-I think I'd prefer to be called partner..."

"Hm? You would?" Ranta asked.

It pissed Haruhiro off to see Ranta getting carried away like that, but Moguzo looked a lot more relaxed than before.

Haruhiro was relieved, too. Without any hyperbole, Moguzo was the core of the party. It was no exaggeration to say that whether the party could perform well or not depended on Moguzo. So long as Moguzo was fine, things probably wouldn't change even if Haruhiro wasn't around. Basically, it was all a question of how best to use Moguzo.

"Hey, now!" Bri-chan called, clapping his hands. "All of you darlings, pay attention! Gather around me, right now! I'm going to give a rundown of the plan! Okay? Quickly now! Hurry, scurry!"

Grimgar
of
Fantasy and Ash

9. To My Little Kittens

"...And that's about the sum of it."

Bri-chan had a cleft chin. Not just a slight cleft, either: it was a deep, clear cleft. His lips were dark black. He probably wore black lipstick. If they were that color without lipstick, he'd be a monster. He had a lot of eyelashes and they were fluttery. Were those natural? His cheeks were red. It looked like he wore rouge. Actually, he wore way too much makeup.

Today's Bri-chan was fully clad in armor and had a sword at his hip. He still wriggled when he moved, though. Scary.

His armor had the hexagram carved into it, so was he a paladin like Brigadier General Wren Water?

Bri-chan had a strange sparkle in his light blue eyes, and his hips were swaying. "The area outside of Deadhead Watching Keep is as I was just saying. To quickly review, camps centered around towers are dotted around the area near the fortress. In each of these camps there are two to five orcs. Well, I think most of you here would know, but since a handful of you look like you don't, I'll say this just to be

113

sure. These camps and the keep itself are collectively called Deadhead Watching Keep. Everyone follow me so far? Any questions? No? None, right? It'd be a problem for me if there were. Anyway, next I'll talk about the keep itself."

Bri-chan spread out a map on the ground, illuminating it with a lamp. It looked like a map of the main keep at Deadhead Watching Keep. He now pointed at it.

"The walls surrounding the keep are around six meters high on the south side, where the main gate is. They're lower on the east and west sides, about four meters high. On the north side with the rear gate, they're around five meters. If we're going to go over the walls and get into the keep, we have to use the exterior stairs to go up to the roof. There's no entrance on the first floor, you see. So, the entrance is here," Bri-chan said, using the tip of his sheathed sword to point at a spot on the roof.

"I'm sure you can tell just by looking," he continued, "but it's built so that the southeast corner of the wall is connected to the keep. The exterior stairs are on the east side, way towards at the south, see? In short, even if we go in through the main gate at the south, we'll have to go almost the entire way around clockwise to reach the stairs. So, if we race up the stairs and go inside through the roof entrance, now we'll have to go all the way back down to the first floor. You all realize why it's been designed in such a cumbersome way, right? For defense, of course. Once we go all the way down to the first floor, there are more stairs going up to the watch towers in the northwest, southwest, and northeast.

"...Ah, right, right, I should say this for our rookies' benefit. This keep has three watch towers sticking up out of it. That's where the

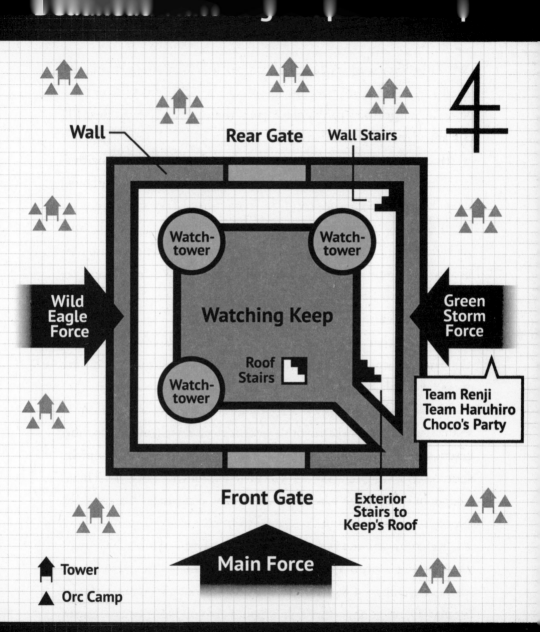

4

Wall — | Rear Gate | Wall Stairs

Watch-tower | Watch-tower

Wild Eagle Force | Watching Keep | Green Storm Force

Roof Stairs

Watch-tower

Team Renji
Team Haruhiro
Choco's Party

Front Gate | Exterior Stairs to Keep's Roof

Main Force

Tower
Orc Camp

SPECIAL NOTES

- There are orc camps centered around towers in the area surrounding the fortress, each of which holds two to five orcs.

- The walls surrounding the keep are roughly six meters high on the southern side where the main gate is, roughly four meters high on the western and eastern sides, and roughly five meters high on the

'Watching Keep' part of the name comes from. We anticipate that the enemy boss, the keeper, will be in one of these three towers. Do you have the image down in your head, for the most part?"

Haruhiro nodded a little, still staring intently at the map. They were going to attack this place soon? Somehow, it just didn't feel real.

"Next, for an outline of the operation." Bri-chan began playing with his sword with one hand. It was a fairly heavy sword, but he handled it easily. "We will begin the attack at dawn. The main force will attack the main gate, while the detached force will split into two groups to handle the east and west sides. Okay, you there, don't get scared! It's fine. Because the detached force's role is purely to keep the enemy in check and to act as a diversion.

"The detached force will move first. We will begin the attack from the east and west. When the enemy tries to defend themselves, the main force will rush up to the main gate and quickly break through. I said we'd be splitting into two groups, right? Twenty parties will go to the east. I'll be commanding this group, so we'll call them the Green Storm Force. You get it, right? Their name comes from my fabulous hair color. Seventeen parties will go west, and I'll leave Kajiko in charge of them. So, their name will be the Wild Eagle Force. Well? Not bad, don't you think?"

Kajiko raised one eyebrow. "Yes. It's not bad."

"I've already thought about how the forces will be divided," Bri-chan said. "Okay? I'll just point out who's in the Green Storm Force. Ready? Okay, you, and you, you, you, you, you, you, you, you, you, you, you, you, you, you, you, you, and then, Renji."

"Yeah," Renji said.

"Your party is with me. Disappointed, aren't you, Kajiko?"

"Who's disappointed?" Kajiko glared at Bri-chan. "Are you looking to get killed, Britney?"

"Heavens, no. If I got killed, I wouldn't be able to take good men in my arms, now would I?" Bri-chan said, showering Renji with his passionate gaze. "Right? Rennnji!"

Renji was completely impassive. If he could stay expressionless after a look like that from Bri-chan, that was amazing all by itself. Even Haruhiro, who wasn't involved, had gotten goosebumps from it. To be blunt, that look had been repulsive.

Bri-chan let out a disturbing giggle before turning to look at Haruhiro. "Also, you."

"...Ah. Yes, sir," Haruhiro said.

"Lastly," Bri-chan said, pointing at Mr. Pleasant from Choco's party. "You. That's twenty parties. The rest of you are in Kajiko's Wild Eagle Force. Understood?"

The volunteer soldiers each gave their own response. It didn't sound like anyone was going to object. Even if they didn't like it, it'd have taken a lot of bravery to stand up to Bri-chan. After all, he was terrifyingly creepy.

"Kajiko, you have a timepiece, right?" Bri-chan asked.

"Yeah," Kajiko said, pulling a sparkling silver pocket watch from her chest and showing it to him.

"Oh, my." Bri-chan looked like he'd been about to display what looked like a pocket watch in his hand, but had thought better of it. "That's a nice piece you have there, darling. Oh, gosh. Mine just seems like a piece of junk in comparison."

Kajiko laughed nasally. "The truth is, it is a piece of junk, isn't it?"

"Oh, you do have a mouth on you," Bri-chan said. "It's old, so it's expensive, you know? I have my doubts about its accuracy, though. Anyway, if you have a watch, the timing should be fine. I'll tell you what the starting time is later. Now then, how the operation will progress. Once the operation begins, we take whatever camps we come across as we advance towards the walls. Crush any camp that has orcs in it. If we dawdle, the orcs may come out of their camps to surround us, so crush them as fast as you can manage. That is the first stage."

Moguzo gave a powerful nod. He really should've conserved his energy, though, so that he didn't get too psyched up.

Bri-chan used his sword to point at the wall. "The second stage is when we reach the walls and launch our attack. The enemy will likely respond with archers, but according to the thief team sent out as scouts, there's around 200 orcs on guard. Their numbers aren't that impressive, so there's no need to be scared. That said, if you get hit in the wrong place, it could kill you instantly. We've prepared shields, so..." Bri-chan gestured with his chin towards a pile of board-like objects piled up at the side of the road. "Before we set out, each of you take one. You can treat these shields as expendable."

"Well, that's generous!" Ranta gave him a big grin, but Bri-chan ignored him.

"...Anyway, we'll be attacking a wall with no gates, so we'll be putting up ladders to climb right over. Of course, we've prepared the ladders for that, as well. On that note, we need people on ladder duty. Their job will be to carry the ladders until we arrive on site, assemble them, and raise them against the walls. My Green Storm Force and the Wild Eagle Force will each have four ladders. While I'll let Kajiko decide who her ladder teams will be, the ones to have the honor of being the ladder team for our Green Storm Force will be..."

Haruhiro had a bad feeling.

He didn't know why, but every time he had a good feeling about something he turned out to be wrong and if he had a bad feeling, it was guaranteed to be right.

This time was no exception.

Bri-chan pointed at Haruhiro, then to Mr. Pleasant, one after the other. "Your party and your party will do it."

"Whaaaaaaaaaaaaaaaaaaaaaaaaaa?" Ranta screwed up his face until his lips rolled back. "Why do we have to do it? We already have to carry shields! Like we can carry big, heavy ladders on top of that!"

...Ranta, man, you've got guts.

Before Haruhiro could say anything, Bri-chan drew his sword and pointed the tip of it at Ranta's throat. "*I* am the commander here. You don't like it? Leave. After returning your advance, of course, okay?"

"...I-I'm not giving back the money! Actually... I can't." Ranta lowered his eyes, letting out a little laughing snort. "...Already spent it all."

Haruhiro nearly fell over. "Already?!"

"Oh, shove it! It was money I earned, so it was mine! I was free to do whatever I wanted with it!"

"Well, yes, but..."

"Well then," Bri-chan tucked his sword point under Ranta's chin, giving him a little poke. "Do as you're told. If you disobey me and try to run off, you'll be a fugitive from that moment onward."

"A fugitive...?! Th-that's so cool! Wait, no, it sounds like it might be a little dangerous...?"

Shihoru shook her head back and forth. "...Not 'might.'"

The look Merry gave him was reminiscent of an ice statue. "It's absolutely dangerous."

"Now, listen here," Bri-chan pulled back his sword and gave it a little spin. "The ladder team has a *very* important job, you know? They have to do everything they can to avoid combat before we reach the fortress, but when the time comes, they charge up to the walls and raise the ladders with a bang. It's a cool job."

"...Cool," Ranta repeated the word to himself, as if carefully considering it, then his face broke into an ugly smirk. "Well, if that's how it is, you know? There's no other choice. Guess we'll do it. I mean, for such an important job, you've got to be as big a man as me, or it's just not gonna happen, right?"

"We'll be doing it, too, though," Mr. Tall from Choco's party said, openly taking a shot at Ranta.

"Shut up!" Ranta said, glaring hard at Mr. Tall. "That's one thing, this is another! Besides, you're my junior, dammit! Don't get in the way when your senior is having a good time, octopus-brain!"

"I'm not an octopus."

"What are you, a squid, then?!"

"...Fine. Whatever."

"Wahahahahahahahahahahahahahaha! I won! Victory is mine!"

Ms. Short Hair from Choco's party was looking at Ranta the way one might look at a cockroach from a distance. "...You're the worst."

Haruhiro covered his face with his hands. "Please, don't embarrass us any more..."

Regardless, Haruhiro and Choco's parties needed to carry four ladders. He'd have liked to play the reliable senior and take one more than they did, but that wasn't going to be possible. Two ladders each seemed reasonable.

The ladders were long. By combining two ladders that were a little over two meters long, they'd create super long ladders that were over four meters long. In other words, they actually needed to transport eight ladders that were each a little over two meters long.

Haruhiro, Ranta, and Moguzo would each take one. The three girls would take one between them. That seemed about right.

Choco's party was composed of four guys and two girls, so it looked like the guys would each be carrying one.

They needed to carry the shields in addition to this, so they were all looking at some rather heavy labor. Somehow, it felt like they were going to be exhausted before they even arrived.

"Now then," Bri-chan said, bending over and thrusting his butt out. "Entering the fortress and sweeping it clean of enemies is primarily supposed to be the job of the main force, but I'll go over the enemy's forces just so that you're all aware. As I said before, we anticipate 200 orcs, the majority of them belonging to a clan called the Zesh. They dye their hair black and have red tattoos on their faces. Their equipment is mostly standardized, too. They use a sword with a single-edged blade called a gahari, shields with fur on them, and red helmets, as well as a bow and arrow. As you'd expect from a group that's come to the front line, the Zesh clan are not weak. However, the orcs in the camps are of various clans, and the bonds between them shouldn't be strong."

The challenge would come in the time it took to get the ladders up on the wall. The detached force's job would be to keep the enemy in check, to be a diversion. If they put up the long ladders and made it so they could climb the walls, that'd make the enemy worried.

When you thought of it that way, being on the ladder team really was a big responsibility. They had to avoid battles, or, in other words, they didn't have to fight, which was probably why the job had been given to volunteer soldiers as low down as Haruhiro and Choco's parties, but, if they failed, it'd mean big trouble.

"The keeper is Zoran Zesh of the Zesh Clan," Bri-chan said. "Zoran-chan is well-built enough that you should be able to tell it's him at a glance. We have intel saying he fights with a two-sword style. The twenty or so orcs who're Zoran-chan's closest associates are all supposed to be very skilled. On top of that, it looks like there are a small number of sorcerers. Orcish sorcerers are lightly equipped. They don't wear armor or helmets, so they're easy to pick out, but I think a good number of you will never have faced one, so be careful. Orcish sorcery is centered around psychokinesis and insects. It's quite different from magic: they don't chant spells or make elaborate gestures, so it's quick. They're dangerous, so if you see a sorcerer, prioritize taking them out. Other than that... Right, right, the smoke signals."

Yume tilted her head to the side. "Smoking kills?"

"Yes, someone's collapsed...they're coughing up blood. Now they aren't breathing. Could it be...they're dead?! Who could the culprit be?! Who was it?! This was caused by—Wait, no, that's not what we're talking about! Gosh! Look what you made me go along with! What are you going to do about it? Nobody even laughed!" Bri-chan shouted.

"Could it be you're gettin' mad at Yume? Maybe?" Yume asked.

"...I'm not mad. There's no way I'd *ever* be so petulant, is there?"

"You aren't, huh?" Yume said. "Oh, but, Bri-chan, sorry. Yume, she might've gone and done that thing. She may've detailed the conversation."

"Listen now, we don't have time for you to detail the conversation," Bri-chan said. "You have to *derail* it. Well, no, you don't have to do that, okay?"

"If Yume doesn't have to do that, what should she be doin'? Yume wonders about that."

"Let it go! Just close your mouth and let me talk! I don't mind girls like you, but you're throwing me off balance here, so be quiet! Please! Zip your lips!"

"Zip."

"Okay. Now, back to the smoke signals. When Deadhead Watching Keep is under a large scale attack, they use smoke signals to alert Riverside Iron Fortress. I'm sure the signal will go up right away this time, too. But, the attack will be starting over there at the same time. Even if they call for them, reinforcements won't come. That's why you shouldn't panic even if you do see a signal go up. Well, that's about it, I suppose. I know I've talked a lot, but as long as we don't make some incredible blunder, we should be able to win this. The keeper, and the bounty on any famous sorcerers, will likely have nothing to do with our detached force. Either way, it's not going to be a difficult battle. You kids without much experience can put your minds at ease, too."

Bri-chan seemed to be directing those words at Haruhiro and his group specifically. Even if they couldn't put their minds at ease, Haruhiro was starting to feel that it might not be as bad as he'd thought. Just maybe, carrying some ladders and shields the six kilometers from here to Deadhead Watching Keep would be their biggest difficulty.

"That said!" Bri-chan went on, suddenly taking on a dangerous tone. "We're up against our natural enemies. With No-Life King dead and gone and the undead suppressed, the orcs are the largest faction in the frontier. Let your guard down, and you won't get off with just a slap on the wrist. You could die quite easily, you know?"

Haruhiro gulped.

Boost them up, then let them down. That was what Bri-chan was doing, huh?

Still, it might be an effective strategy. In fact, Haruhiro had been getting a little optimistic, so being knocked down from that high had put him in a good state of readiness, both mentally and physically.

Bri-chan's pink tongue licked his black lips. "Well, there you have it. Get your butts in gear and let's go, my little kittens."

10. Graduation

Soon, the dawn would come.

No one was speaking. Nobody so much as stirred. Even when they breathed, they did their best to stifle it.

Yet there was that idiot, Ranta, covering his mouth with his hands, shaking his body back and forth.

Is it a sneeze, maybe? Haruhiro thought. *He's about to sneeze, and he's trying to hold it back? You're kidding me. What the hell is he doing?*

Aw, crap.

Not good.

He's gonna blow.

He so is.

...No.

Looks like he managed to hold back. Haruhiro let out a sigh of relief. *Thank goodness.*

In that moment, it must've come back.

"Achoo!"

A few dozen glares stabbed into Ranta over his inability to hold in a sneeze.

Yet Ranta, when he looked to the other volunteer soldiers around them, gave a gesture that was less an apology and more an "Oh, just calm down."

He doesn't feel guilty in the least. What's wrong with him?

Haruhiro poked his head out from behind a pile of scrap wood, looking at the camps here and there.

The camps generally had one tower and one, two, sometimes three tents. On top of some towers, there was an orc, but not always.

It didn't look like there was any movement. The sound of that sneeze must not have reached them. They were safe.

The sun wasn't up yet, but it was already pretty bright.

The Green Storm Force led by Britney, or Bri-chan, was to the east of Deadhead Watching Keep. They were laying low in what seemed to be the remains of a camp, at least judging by the lumber, cloth, and stones lying around.

Orc camps were attacked by volunteer soldiers, destroyed, and then rebuilt. It was something that had happened time and again, so there were plenty of places like this one to hide in. Even so, Haruhiro was beside himself with worry that the orcs might find them any moment now.

He was feeling restless and impatient, too. Having to wait like this, it was tough. He wished it'd just start already. He'd feel better that way.

He could see the keep in the distance, the three towers rising from it ominously, like horns. The walls were made of stone, with some black substance having been used to fill the gaps. Red paint had been used to write letters, or to draw symbols of some sort on it. The towers were covered in jagged metal and wood, but that didn't seem to be decorative. They might have been aiming to make it a more effective defense that way.

The east and west walls were four meters high, right? Haruhiro thought. *That's not crazy high, but we won't be able to climb over them if they're like that. Yeah, looks like the ladders are going to be necessary after all.*

The camp towers were decorated with animal skulls, as well as dried severed heads on pikes that hadn't rotted away to become skulls yet.

Looks like there are human skulls and heads in the mix, too. That's where the name Deadhead comes from, huh? I don't want to end up like that, he thought, suddenly. *Nah, I'm not going to, okay?*

Haruhiro checked how the ladder he was carrying felt. It'd been pretty heavy to carry. Not so much the weight, as how bulky it had been. The shield he was carrying to block arrows was tied to his back with a string. It was getting in the way, too.

Then, Bri-chan stood up.

Bri-chan was looking at his golden pocket watch. He nodded. He raised one hand.

It was finally time. Haruhiro waited with bated breath.

Bri-chan swung his hand down. "Begin the attack!"

At the same time, they heard cheering. From the main force, maybe? Or was it Wild Eagle Force?

"Charge! Destroy the camps!" Bri-chan shouted.

As soon as Bri-chan shouted the order, volunteer soldiers emerged from the mountain of scrap one after another, quickly attacking the orc camps.

"L-let's go! We need to go, too!" Haruhiro cried, his voice shrill.

He lifted up the ladder, advancing along with the very rear of Green Storm Force.

"O Light, may Lumiaris' divine protection be upon you... Protection!" Merry cast a spell. A shining hexagram appeared on his left wrist, making his body feel lighter.

What about the others? They had them, too.

Haruhiro was trying to run, but he was slow. He blamed the ladder. Man, it was hard to run with this thing.

Ahh. You know, maybe I'm feeling pretty tense? For a moment, he forgot what he was doing. *Is Choco all right? Where is she? I don't have time to worry about that, huh?*

Still, everyone sure was amazing. The orcs were dropping like flies. Was that Arve magic?

The tents were on fire. There were even volunteer soldiers knocking the towers down. The camps were being captured right before his eyes.

How far had the guys at the very front gotten? He couldn't see them, so he didn't really know. He doubted they could've made it to the wall yet, though.

Just maybe, we ought to be hurrying a bit more? Though, we can't do what we can't do.

"There're smoke signals going up!" he heard Merry shout. When he turned to look, Merry was pointing towards the fortress.

There were thin trails of thick grey smoke rising from the three towers. A call for reinforcements. However, Riverside Iron Fortress should have been under attack now, too. Reinforcements wouldn't be coming.

"Waaaay off in the distance, there's smoke goin' up, too!" Yume said.

It was true.

There were a few smoke trails to the west, too.

What could it mean? Was it one of those things? A relay? There might have been places other than Deadhead Watching Keep to raise smoke signals.

It was around 40 kilometers from here to Riverside, so they might not be able to see them from there otherwise. But, wait, the smoke trails, didn't it seem like they were going up two at a time?

That was it. He understood. It wasn't just Deadhead. Riverside also raised a signal when they were attacked. That had to be it: both sides were trying to communicate to the other that they were under attack.

Still, if that were the case, it'd mean the orcs at Deadhead now knew they couldn't count on reinforcements from Riverside. If they'd thought reinforcements were coming, the orcs would've been likely to try to keep their losses to a minimum and bide their time until they arrived.

If not, then what would they do? Wouldn't they desperately resist, mad with the fear of death?

Well, the higher-ups had no doubt thought about all of this. It was nothing for the rank and file to worry about. Haruhiro and the others just had to do their own jobs properly.

In other words, ladder duty.

Once their allies crushed the camps, they had to get the ladders up on the walls. It looked like the camps around them had been destroyed already.

Choco's party was behind them. They were going slower than Haruhiro's.

We can go now, he thought.

He was quickly proven wrong. It wasn't going to be so easy. And, hold on...

Who let these guys get by? There are orcs. Two of them. Coming our way.

Well, not so much our *way.*

They were heading in the direction of Choco's party.

"O-orcs!" he shouted. "T-two, incoming...!"

When Haruhiro raised his voice to warn them, Choco's party stopped—

Wait, what? What're you stopping for?

It seemed they didn't know themselves.

"Ah!"

"Oh, crap!"

"Whoa, the ladder...!"

Not good. This is pretty bad. They're hopeless.

Choco's party was confused and panicking. There was no way they could either run or put up a proper fight like that.

"We can't afford to lose half the ladders!" Haruhiro called. "We have to help them! Let's take on the orcs ourselves! We'll set down our ladders and shields for now!"

"Y-yeah!" Moguzo shouted, letting his ladder drop to the ground and taking the shield off his back.

"Sure thing!" Ranta was always quick at times like this. "It's finally time! To graduate! I'm losing my virginity!"

"Umph!" Shihoru picked up the shield Yume had discarded and put it together with her own.

Merry laid the ladder down at her feet, nodding to Haruhiro.

"Conserve your magic for now!" Haruhiro shouted as he ran forward.

First, he needed to get a feel for the orcs' strength. There was a possibility that they had a long fight ahead of them, after all.

Slipping in between Choco's confused party, Moguzo slashed at Orc A and Ranta charged towards Orc B. For equipment, the orcs had some sort of scaled armor, a helmet that covered everything but their faces, and some hefty swords. The hair poured out from their helmets. Yellow for Orc A, red for Orc B. Their skin was green.

Haruhiro signaled to Yume with his eyes, then they tried to flank or get behind Orc B.

Man, orcs sure are big.

Their height wasn't all that impressive. They were taller than Haruhiro, but still shorter than Moguzo. Still, they were much thicker and wider. To use a little hyperbole, they looked like they were twice as big as a human.

Taking their whole body into consideration, they were a full size larger than Moguzo. Moguzo was a big guy, standing 186 centimeters tall, and they were a full size bigger than him. What was more, these were probably average orcs.

They said that orcs were the largest faction in the frontier of Grimgar, and Haruhiro could believe it. They looked tough, and it wasn't all show; they actually were strong.

Ranta was, of course, being pushed back by Orc B, so he used Exhaust to go straight backwards and run like crazy. When he did that, naturally, Orc B chased after Ranta.

Haruhiro and Yume would have to chase Orc B, so there was no way they had time to be getting beside or behind him.

It was hard to say that Moguzo was winning, either. He was taking a lot of slash attacks, but somehow managing to block them with his armor. Though, that was still defending against them, so in some ways, you could have called it an even fight. From the looks of things, Orc A was at a slight advantage.

Muscle strength, huh?

It was the way they were built. Orcs had stronger muscles than humans. Muscle didn't just affect their arm strength; it affected their leg strength, too. The more muscle they had, even if it made them heavier, the faster they could run and the higher they could jump. Being big didn't necessarily mean being slow. Even agility was affected by the muscles, after all.

The orcs had smushed noses, large mouths, and boar-like tusks. From Haruhiro's human perspective, they weren't pretty. Though, hideous as they might have been, they didn't look especially unintelligent. From the assembly of the towers and designs of the tents, it was more than apparent that they were intelligent.

Haruhiro thought displaying skulls and severed heads on the towers like that was barbaric, but the humans and orcs were in conflict. If the orcs were doing that to intimidate humans, it wasn't like he couldn't understand why.

The orcs were superior to humans physically, and it was hard to say which side was more intelligent. In that case, when it came to simple combat potential, weren't orcs stronger than humans?

"Don't be intimidated!" Merry shouted. "Once you get used to it, you can fight them!"

She's right, he thought. *At the very least, we have to think that way. If we lose in spirit, even fights we should be able to win will become unwinnable.*

"Merry's right!" he shouted. "We aren't used to how orcs move yet, that's all! Moguzo, you can do it! There's no way you can't!"

"Muh…!" Moguzo went on the attack. Or rather, he used a skill. A heavy armor combat skill, Steel Guard.

Moguzo deliberately used his armor to knock back Orc A's sword. Then, while Orc A was off balance, he slammed The Chopper into him. Even when the orc defended, he pounded it into him.

Seeing Orc A faltering, Orc B's footwork became more cautious.

Haruhiro's eyes met Ranta's.

"You don't have to tell me!" Ranta shouted.

Even when Orc B closed in, Ranta didn't run away with Exhaust. Orc B had closed in less intensely than before.

"There!"

It was Reject.

Ranta pushed Orc B back, immediately stepping in after him.

"Anger…!"

I thought it was a good thrust, too.

Orc B twisted and avoided it.

But he only barely dodged it. It was close. Ranta almost had him.

"I know! I'm unbeatable!" Ranta called.

"Since when?!" Haruhiro shouted.

His back.

Orc B had its back to Haruhiro. He couldn't see that line.

He went for a Spider, but the orc noticed him at the last moment and avoided it. But Haruhiro wasn't alone.

"There! Ha!" Yume attacked with a combo of Brush Clearer and Diagonal Cross.

Orc B knocked Yume's machete aside with a loud clang and tried to go for a counterattack.

"Hanyaa!" Yume rolled away like a pit rat.

Orc B tried to go after her immediately, but, again, Yume wasn't alone.

"Hey, hey, hey!" Ranta swung his longsword around wildly. He was practically throwing himself at Orc B.

Meanwhile, Yume got back into a fighting posture. Haruhiro was looking to get behind the orc, too. Orc B had less and less leeway to work with. He was definitely feeling pressed. They just needed one more push.

That push came.

"Thanks...!" Moguzo slammed a Thanks Slash into Orc A's shoulder.

Orc A didn't go down, but he was unsteady. He couldn't wield his sword properly. It was only a matter of time.

Orc B was confused and panicking.

Haruhiro was right behind Orc B, so he couldn't see his expression. Still, it was readily apparent how flustered he was.

Backstab.

Silently closing the distance, Haruhiro slid the dagger in smoothly. Considering that he couldn't see the line, the dagger's blade broke through Orc B's scale armor easily and struck flesh.

That wasn't a fatal strike, he thought to himself.

Still, it was good enough.

When Haruhiro leapt back, Yume struck Orc B twice, three times with her machete. The machete was shorter than a longsword, but it still had a good amount of weight to it. It didn't manage to cut through, but the blunt force should've done a decent amount of damage.

Orc B reeled.

"Hatred!" When Ranta leapt in from outside Orc B's reach, the orc couldn't avoid it.

The shoulder. Ranta's longsword hit, but it slid across Orc B's armor with a screech.

Was that intentional?

Ranta didn't cut open the tough scale armor, instead aiming for the face with a flick of his wrist.

Still, that result had to have been pure chance. I can't believe he did it intentionally.

Ranta's longsword severed the chin strap holding the helmet on Orc B's head, then got caught on the helmet. The helmet came off.

"Ta-dah!" Ranta was wearing a blackened bascinet. He had the visor lowered, so his face was hidden, but he was probably sticking his tongue out right now.

Ranta used his longsword not so much to cut Orc B as to slug him. He slugged him like crazy.

Orc B wasn't able to stand for long. Even when he went down, Ranta showed no mercy. He didn't even try to stop.

Moguzo used a second Thanks Slash to cut down Orc A. Orc B wasn't moving anymore. Once that happened, Ranta finally stopped.

Choco and her group looked horrified. Even so, Haruhiro didn't criticize Ranta. It hadn't been pleasant to watch, but Ranta hadn't been wrong in what he'd done. Even if it was cruel, he was right to finish off the enemy. And living creatures could be so tenacious. Though they'd die so easily when their time came, sometimes they'd launch a fierce counterattack even after taking a deadly blow.

"Heh, heh, heh..." Ranta raised his longsword aloft. "I got my vice!

Finally, I graduated from being a virgin! Congratulations, me!"

Yeah, he's right, isn't he? Haruhiro thought. *And with no casualties, to boot. Merry and Shihoru didn't even have to use magic.*

"Yay!" Yume cried, jumping into the air. "Yume and everyone, we're kinda amazin', huh?!"

Ranta let out an obnoxious laugh. "Your tits are so tiny, they don't shake even when you jump around, huh? —Yow. You didn't have to punch me!"

"You said somethin' that deserved a punchin'," Yume told him.

Moguzo pumped his arm with a "Yeah!" and nodded to himself.

Shihoru had a hesitant, but still seemingly happy smile on her face.

Merry looked relieved.

It wasn't that Haruhiro didn't feel something welling up inside him, too. He did. It started at his fingertips, tickling Haruhiro's heart and turning it upside down, then rising to his head and intoxicating him. Honestly, for a while, he basked in it.

"...Awesome," Mr. Pleasant from Choco's party mumbled.

"Those're our senpais for you," said Laughing Man. The words could've been read as sarcastic, but it seemed that wasn't his intent.

"Y-you saved us..." Mr. Priest was sitting on the ground. It looked like he'd been pretty scared.

"Wow..." Ms. Short Hair said, looking a little out of it.

Choco was looking at Haruhiro. Like Ms. Short Hair, she was dazed. Her mouth was slightly agape.

It wasn't a bad feeling.

Then, Mr. Tall went and ruined it. "Well, there're people killing orcs all over the place, though."

"*Heyyyyyyyyyyyyyyyyyyyyy!*" Ranta pointed his orc-blood-soaked longsword at Mr. Tall. "Listen, pal! Don't go killing a guy's buzz when he's feeling proud of himself! Who do you think you are? Old Man Buzzkill?"

"...I'm not that old," the man said. "And who's that supposed to be? Who's Old Man Buzzkill?"

"Like I should know!" Ranta flared.

"You're the one who said it."

"Shut up! Just shut up! Just because you're a little tall doesn't mean...!"

"Ranta! Enough!" Haruhiro barked.

Mr. Tall had Haruhiro annoyed too, but this wasn't the time to be getting full of themselves. Haruhiro raced back to where they'd dropped the ladders and their shields.

"We've got to go! We're the ladder team!" he shouted.

Hurriedly strapping the shield to his back, he picked his ladder up once more. There were already a not-insignificant number of volunteer soldiers closing in on the wall.

Haruhiro and the party ran. They ran.

Choco's party was following them.

The camps they passed were all uninhabited. All that they saw in them were orc corpses.

He thought he heard Yume say, "Ow...!" but that wasn't it. She'd actually said "Arrows...!"

The orcs had formed a line on the wall, bows and arrows at the ready. No, not just at the ready. They were firing.

"Oh, crap!" Haruhiro shouted. "Shields! There're arrows! Everyone, get your shields up...!"

The arrows rained down. Haruhiro used his shield like an umbrella. It was difficult to carry the ladder while holding a shield, but he had no choice. While there weren't that many arrows, sometimes one would come their way. If they took a hit, it might kill them.

"Ladders! Hurry!" the volunteer soldiers by the wall were shouting.

"All right!" Ranta shouted, but Haruhiro stopped him before he could charge.

"We've got to assemble them first!" Haruhiro shouted.

"Oh! That's right!"

"Merry, Yume, Shihoru, use the shields!" Haruhiro called.

He had the three of them line up with their shields next to each other, and assembled the ladders behind them. He had to fit the ladders together and pound the nails in. His hands were shaking. An arrow pierced one of the shields, and Shihoru let out a little shriek. Haruhiro couldn't find the strength to do it.

"Give me that!" Moguzo snatched the hammer from Haruhiro, pounding the nails in one after another. He tried pushing and pulling on the ladder.

It's good to go—I think, Haruhiro thought.

"Okay, let's go!" he called.

The completed ladders were more than four meters long. They couldn't be carried by one person. Haruhiro and Ranta formed a team, taking one of the ladders, while Moguzo and Yume formed a team and took the other.

The orcs were desperate. As they got closer to the wall, the number of arrows increased. The intensity continued to build. Arrows stabbed through their shields.

Hey, wait—aren't we being targeted here?! Haruhiro thought.

"Ohhhhhh, crap, crap, crap, crap!" he shouted.

"Whoooooooooa! This is scary!" Ranta yelled.

"Hunnnnnnnnngh...!" Moguzo grunted.

"Eeeeeeeek!" Yume screamed.

"...E-everyone, do your best...!" Shihoru called.

"It's fine! We've got shields!" Merry hollered.

Don't stop, Haruhiro thought. *We can't stop. If we stop walking for even a second, we probably won't be able to move forward anymore. All at once. We have to do this all at once.*

While screaming something in a loud voice, they charged forward, feeling like they might trip at any moment, then brought the ladder up on the spiky wall.

The volunteer soldiers roared as one. The air shook and trembled. It was like a cry of victory. The rush was even more intense than when Haruhiro had killed the orc.

How's that? How's that?! I did it! I really did it! Look! Look at that! Is this what they call a rush of endorphins?

"Move...!" Renji shoved Haruhiro aside. He was trying to climb the ladder. He didn't have a shield. Even though there were orcs with bows right above.

Isn't he afraid? Haruhiro thought. *That takes some serious guts.*

"Hold on, Renji!" they heard Bri-chan shout. "There's no need to be in such a rush!"

Again, the air shook and trembled.

It didn't come from here this time, Haruhiro thought. *Where did it come from? Was it Wild Eagle Force on the west wall? Or was it—either way, those weren't human voices. They were probably orcs. An angry roar. That mass of sound made the heavens and earth rumble. Could it have been...*

"From the main gate?!" Haruhiro screamed.

11. Warriors of the Frontier

His name was Anthony Justeen.

A proud warrior of the renowned Alterna Frontier Army 1st Brigade Warrior Regiment.

He was not just any old warrior. He was a master warrior.

Anthony had placed his honor as a warrior on the line, participating in Operation "Two-Headed Snake" in the glorious position of Platoon Commander. He was attacking Deadhead Watching Keep head-on, trying to take it fair and square.

Of course, if a warrior as great as Anthony was going to grace the battlefield, he belonged at the very front. At this very moment, he was leading his manly subordinates as they pressed towards the keep, but, in his heart, there was one thing that he found somewhat unpleasant.

Wren Water.

That gutless milksop. Who'd made *him* a paladin? Who'd made *him* a brigadier general? He was a mainland-born sissy.

A proper paladin would stand at the front of his army, putting his life on the line to protect his comrades. At least, a frontier-born paladin with a backbone would, but that rotten paladin and fake brigadier general wasn't like that. He had a hundred paladins and a handful of priests there guarding him while he sat smugly at the rear of the main force.

He was a fool. A damn fool and a coward. He was shit. *This* was supposed to be the scion of the famous Water family?

Like Anthony cared. Wren could go die. Die and rot.

Even if it was a given that General Graham Rasentra would be the one to lead the attack on Riverside Iron Fortress, ordinarily, the frontier-born, frontier-bred warrior among warriors, Brigadier General Ian Ratty, should've been the one to lead this main force of incomparable power to conquer Deadhead Watching Keep. Wren Water should have stayed in Alterna, crying and trembling like the freshly-hatched chick that he was.

In fact, even now, as Anthony had trampled the orc camps underfoot, pushed up to the walls through the rain of arrows, and was about to put the battering ram to the main gate, that wretch had contributed nothing.

At the beginning, he'd ordered them forward. That was the only thing he'd done. Even a brat could have done that.

The majority of the warriors in the Frontier Army were from the frontier. Frontier-born warriors prided themselves on their gruff manliness and looked down on the feeble mainlanders with utter contempt. That was because the mainlanders had a lot of pride and not much else. Unable to even wield a sword properly, they were a bunch of good-for-nothings entirely deserving of that disdain.

Honestly, from the moment Wren Water had been chosen as their commander, the warriors' morale had sunk. Not to mention that, in this operation, Riverside Iron Fortress was the main objective, so every one of them must've been somewhat disappointed to be assigned to taking Deadhead Watching Keep, a fight it was a given they would win.

Of course, they'd complete their mission. They would take the keep, but Wren Water would take the credit for it. It was unthinkable that this would end in anything but a victory.

Curse Wren Water.

That piece of shit.

So, this was the power of a famous family, was it? Basically, that was what it had to be. He wasn't here because of his talent. Even if he did nothing, the accolades would roll in towards him and accumulate on their own. That was how it was all set up.

The man who could be called the symbol of the Frontier Army, General Rasentra, was turning 46 this year. He was still in the prime of his life, but there were persistent rumors that the mainland might want the general. It was also said he had repeatedly declined requests to take the position of Commander-in-Chief. However, someday, the general would be taken away to the mainland. Could it be that Wren Water was aiming to take his place when he left?

There were currently three brigadier generals who were next in rank after the general in the frontier. Brigadier General Ian Ratty, Wren Water, the piece of shit, and lastly, Brigadier General Jord Horn, who was always at the general's side.

Common sense dictated that Brigadier General Horn would be the general's successor, but they were much too close for that. The general might want to take Brigadier General Horn back to the mainland with him. If that were to happen, Brigadier General Ratty would be the next general.

In terms of talent, there was no doubt that was how it should have been, but Wren Water was a piece of shit, so he might be plotting to seize the position through the influence of his family.

It was possible. It wasn't impossible, but with that piece of shit being a piece of shit, he might have just wanted to get back to the mainland as quickly as possible.

He was welcome to go. *Hurry up and leave. Shit belongs in a world full of shit,* Anthony thought.

On the other side of the Tenryu Mountains, in the mainland that Anthony had yet to see, there were tens, hundreds of human cities. The countryside spread out as far as the eye could see, and there were cattle leisurely grazing everywhere. There were barbarians in the south that had not yet submitted to the Arabakia Kingdom, but they were no threat. There were occasional wars, but it was rare for soldiers to die.

The barbarians mostly fought among themselves, the kingdom occasionally mediating. The kingdom was like a benevolent father, and the barbarian tribes his children.

Industry had developed in the mainland, and its people loved songs, dance, and music. The blessings of the light god Lumiaris were strong there, filling the land with light. The currency in Alterna was all minted in the mainland, but things that cost one gold in the frontier could be bought for only ten silver in the mainland. The mainland was wealthy. Anything and everything was available there, and if the poor just bowed before the wealthy, they could find food, drink, and clothing. It was said that even the poorest of beggars in the mainland lived better than the soldiers of the frontier.

It's shit, thought Anthony. *It's all a bunch of shit.*

Who did those pieces of shit in the mainland think it was who let them maintain their shitty lifestyles? It was Anthony and warriors like him, shedding blood out in the frontier. If Alterna were ever to fall, the Earth Dragon's Aorta Road under the Tenryu Mountains, which linked the frontier to the mainland, would soon be found. The orcs and undead would come in force to invade the mainland. They'd likely take control of it with ease.

The mainland was built on the sacrifices of Anthony and his men.

It was a tower built on sand.

So, no matter how wonderful the tales they heard of the mainland were, even if it sounded like paradise, it was nothing but shit.

If he were to speak frankly, Anthony wanted to take the place of the orcs and undead, conquer the mainland himself, and pillage it for all it was worth. He had every right to.

Because Anthony had worked hard in his duties, he was defending their property and making them able to amass a fortune. That fortune had been created thanks to Anthony. It was fair to say it was Anthony's fortune.

Of course, he'd never do it.

There was the fact it was an unrealistic goal, but Anthony also had his pride as a warrior. He also liked wine, women, and good food, but those all existed because of men's battlefields. Here in the frontier, there were battles for men.

"Drop dead, Wren Water!" Anthony shouted.

When Anthony shouted that to encourage them, the warriors who were getting ready to swing the battering ram smiled broadly.

"Drop dead, Wren Water!" a warrior agreed.

"Drop dead!"

"Go and drop dead!"

"Drop dead, Wren Water!"

"Drop dead already!"

"Drop dead, Wren Water!"

If the warriors' voices carried back to the rear and Wren Water heard them, there'd be hell to pay later.

Like I care! We'll do our duties. Our duties as warriors. By our warrior pride.

"We'll go on the count of three, two, one!" The warrior in charge of keeping time raised his sword. "Three—"

The rest was drowned out.

There was a roar. A roar fell down on them.

It was orcs.

"Ohhhhhhhhhhhhhhhhhhhhhhhhhhhhhhh sh...!"

Orcs leaped down from the wall. They were falling.

The southern wall was six meters high. It was by no means low. But the orcs were brave. They leapt with no sign of fear, landing on the ground. Some orcs even crushed members of his army as they did.

Mainland-born pieces of shit tended to look down on the orcs and other hostile races, but frontier-born Anthony didn't have that bad habit. He even felt a certain amount of respect for the orcs with their daring and integrity.

Orcs were robust, tenacious, and audacious. They appeared from practically right above the heads of the front line.

Straight at soldiers who had been expecting only arrows, ten—no, likely more than twenty—orcs came swinging, no, *flying* at them.

It was over in an instant. The soldiers trying to man the battering had been mowed down by orcs before they could even register what had happened. While they had let their guard down, who could have predicted that experienced warriors would fall so easily? Still, it was nothing to be surprised about.

The front gate wasn't open yet. Those orcs had launched an assault with no way to return. They were a suicide squad. Death troops.

On the other hand, his men had gone into this operation with the presumption of victory. They'd thought they were guaranteed to win. They'd thought there was no way they could lose. Everyone had thought that.

The enemies were ready to die. Yet his men had had no intention of dying here. It'd made a difference in how ready they were. The difference had been too great.

"Calm down!" Anthony swung at the orc.

Their blades locked, so he went for a Wind. But his opponent knew that was coming. They jostled, then separated.

"Surround them! Surround them! There aren't many of them!"

His subordinates tried to act on Anthony's orders immediately, but many of the warriors were confused and panicking. They couldn't move the way they wanted to.

Then down came the arrows. The confusion deepened and spread.

"We should pull back temporarily!" someone shouted.

"Bullshit!" Anthony shouted while deflecting the orc's slashes. "Have you forgotten your pride as warriors?! Listen here! This is all because of that damned incompetent, Wren Water! It galls me to do it, but we need to wipe his ass for him! We, the warriors of the frontier, will turn this around! Let's do it! Warriors, follow me!"

Grimgar of Fantasy and Ash

12. Later

On the southern wall, where the main gate was, something was very clearly wrong.

What on Earth is happening there? Haruhiro thought. *I've got a bad feeling about this. Actually, I've got nothing but bad feelings about this. Are we in trouble?*

Regardless, Green Storm Force had no choice but to keep assaulting the eastern wall. The enemy was mounting a defense. If they didn't wipe out the orcs on the walls, the rain of arrows was going to make things dangerous.

"First, we take the east wall!" Bri-chan shouted, pointing to the top of the wall with his sword. He wasn't carrying a shield.

It looked like the four ladders had made it to the walls intact. Not just Haruhiro's party, but Choco's party were alive and well, too.

Haruhiro pressed himself up against the wall, holding up his shield. *What's going on up there? I can't see, so I can't tell. Though Renji and the others who went up first must be raising some hell up there. Maybe that's why? Somehow, it feels like the rain of arrows has let up a little compared to before...?*

While he was under his shield, catching his breath, someone grabbed him by the collar.

"Gwah!"

"Hey! Quit wasting time! We're going too, Parupiro!"

It was Ranta. Stupid Ranta. Didn't he realize that hurt?

Haruhiro brushed Ranta's hand aside. "...What're you calling me Parupiro for? And, wait—Huh? Where are we going...?"

"Up the ladders, over the wall! Obviously!"

"No, but..."

"No butts, no farting around, none of your crap! We're going!"

Ranta tried to pull Haruhiro by the arm. *Seriously, give me a break,* Haruhiro thought angrily before tripping Ranta.

"Whoa...?!" Ranta fell over, but quickly jumped to his feet. "You *ass!*"

"Wha...?!" Haruhiro exclaimed. "Man, you're seriously trying to punch me?! At a time like this?!"

"It doesn't matter!" Ranta shouted.

"Yes, it does! If you'd just think about it!"

"I'm the kind of guy who doesn't let common sense get in his way! You could call me a revolutionary!"

"While you're spouting that nonsense, everyone else is going up the ladders!" Haruhiro shot back.

"What'd you say? Whoa! You're serious!"

They could see Choco's group getting ready to climb the ladder. Even Haruhiro was starting to think it'd be best to get moving at this point.

"L-let's get going already!" Moguzo stammered.

When Moguzo said that, Haruhiro made up his mind. "Okay, let's go! Moguzo and I will take the lead! Everyone else, follow after us!"

"You moron! I oughta be first!" Ranta shoved Haruhiro aside and started up the ladder.

"Fine, have it your way...!" Haruhiro fastened his shield to his back, continuing up after Ranta.

Moguzo was going up a different ladder. Yume was behind Haruhiro, while Merry was behind Moguzo. Shihoru came last.

The rain of arrows had already stopped.

It was a chaotic melee up on the walls, but their side had the clear advantage. There were no orcs near Haruhiro and the others.

In a place near the northeast corner of the wall, there were stairs leading down. The enemy looked ready to defend them to the death, but a group centered around Team Renji were pushing them hard.

"Go!" Ranta screamed.

That probably wasn't what caused it, but Renji cut down one orc and kicked another off the wall.

The enemy defense was breaking down, and the volunteer soldiers rushed forth.

"We're going in!" Bri-chan shouted. His voice carried well.

Renji and Ron descended the stairs. The orcs were massed on the stairs, trying to impede their advance.

How are they going to get past that? Haruhiro wondered. *Oh, that's how.*

Renji and Ron rammed themselves into the orcs.

"Push...!" Ron screamed.

No way.

Seriously?

Team Renji and the other volunteer soldiers pushed Renji and Ron from behind. They pushed like crazy.

If you do that, you're going to crush them. They'll be crushed to death.

The orcs tried to push back, but Renji and the others were pushing downwards while they had to push up. Renji and the others had the overwhelming advantage to begin with, but probably having made the first move helped more than anything.

The orcs fell down one after another.

What about Renji and Ron? They were still there.

Well, no, of course they were there, but they were still standing. Renji and Ron stepped over the orcs and headed down.

They'd done it. They made it down the stairs.

"Damn, Renji's awesome!" Ranta bellowed.

I can understand why Ranta's so excited. He's right. You're just too amazing, Renji. To think, those guys came to Grimgar in our group. I don't want to compare us with them. It'll only make me depressed.

Even so, I'm a little bit proud. Those guys are my contemporaries. I want to be able to brag to people about that. I won't do it, though. That'd be depressing in its own way.

Still, you're cool, Renji.

I already knew it, but you're amazing. You're not like us. It's like you're so different, all I can really do is laugh.

"Don't push in too hard! The main force hasn't broken through the front gate yet!" Bri-chan was shouting from on top of the wall as arrows came flying from one of the watchtowers sticking up out of the keep.

Bri-chan knocked one of the arrows out of the air with his sword. He hadn't even been looking in the direction it came from, so it was amazing how easily he'd done it.

Bri-chan didn't have so much as a scratch on him, but there'd been more than a few arrows. A number of volunteer soldiers had been hit and were squatting down.

"It's dangerous to stay here!" Haruhiro shouted loudly enough for Choco's party to hear, as well. "Hurry! It'll probably be safer once we get down off the wall!"

"I know that, you dolt!" Ranta shouted.

Ugh, Ranta, just shut up. You always say too much. Actually, you being here at all is too much. No...restrain myself, I have to restrain myself. Think of it as a trial. The worst kind of trial imaginable.

The watchtowers had been built strong, and they had slits, or tiny windows, to fire arrows out of. Haruhiro's side couldn't see the enemies, so they couldn't tell when they'd fire.

As they were about to head for the stairs, more arrows came. The volunteer soldiers going down them were being targeted.

"Shields!" Haruhiro cried, holding up the shield that had been fastened to his back.

However, none of the others had shields.

"...Huh? Why don't you have shields?" he called.

"Yume, you know, she thought she wouldn't be needin' hers anymore. So, down below, she threw it away. It was heavy, y'know."

"...I-I did that, too," Shihoru admitted.

"M-me, too," Moguzo said.

"Me, too, dammit!" Ranta yelled.

"...Same here," Merry added.

"Urkh... Even Merry did it..." Haruhiro muttered

In fact, he was in the minority. From the looks of it, Choco's party and nearly all of the other volunteer soldiers no longer had their shields.

It seemed Haruhiro's penny-pinching nature had served him well. Though, that said, one shield wasn't going to—

"Ah! We do have shields!" he called. "The orcs' shields!"

As far as he could see, Green Storm Force hadn't taken any serious losses yet, but there were a lot of dead orcs. Along with the corpses and swords, there were shields scattered around, too. They were fur-coated Zesh clan shields.

"Oh! This is just what the doctor ordered!" Ranta cried.

Once Ranta and the others had picked up some shields, the other volunteer soldiers started to imitate them.

They held up their shields towards the watchtowers and rushed onto the stairs. An arrow or two stabbed into the shields, but that was no problem. They were managing to protect themselves just fine.

Halfway down the stairs, the path in front of them became too crowded to move ahead.

In order to get inside the keep, they'd need to ascend the outer stairs and make it to the entrance on the roof. The outside stairs were near the southeast corner of the walls. It would take nearly a full circuit around the outer walls to reach them from the front gate. In fact, the east wall was the closest to them.

Renji and his group were almost at the stairs that went up. However, more and more orcs were piling out of the keep, so even the incredible Team Renji was starting to get slowed down.

"You're doing fabulous! If we keep on pushing, eventually our allies will come!" Bri-chan was shouting things like that as he batted arrows out of the air with his sword, but was this okay?

"...No, it's not!" Haruhiro shouted.

He opened his eyes wide. There were orcs incoming from the north wall where the rear gate was. The main force had attacked from the south and the detached force had attacked from the east and west, so there'd been no one attacking from the north. When they'd learned that enemies had broken through on the east wall, the orcs defending the north wall might have come to reinforce the east wall.

"This is bad!" Haruhiro moaned. "Renji and the others are going to get caught in a pincer!"

"Anyone with hands to spare, go defend against the enemies on the other side!" Bri-chan ordered immediately. A number of parties headed to intercept them at once.

Though, of course, it wasn't going to be that simple. Even if they were going to try to intercept the enemies from the north wall, the area between the stairs down off the wall to the stairs going up the side of the keep was packed with volunteer soldiers. Thanks to that, most of the volunteer soldiers couldn't move very well.

"We'll do it, too!" Mr. Pleasant, the guy who seemed to be the leader of Choco's party, said, jumping down off the wall stairs. Choco and the others looked surprised, but they were about to go after him.

"Hey, wai—" Haruhiro began.

I don't know if you're excited or what, but there are limits to how reckless you can be. There are probably around twenty enemies coming from the north wall. You guys are rookies, okay? Think this through a little.

"Don't we need to go, too?!" Ranta hollered.

When Ranta poked him in the shoulder, Haruhiro hesitated for around two seconds. *Dammit. I can't just watch.*

"Okay, let's go!"

When Haruhiro leapt from the stairs, the battle had already been joined. The orcs' momentum was incredible. In no time flat, a number of volunteer soldiers were taken down.

They're down. Are they dead?

The orcs got past the volunteer soldiers' front line.

Two—no, three—orcs attacked Choco's party.

Mr. Pleasant, Laughing Man, and Mr. Tall each went to take on an orc, but they clearly weren't up to the task.

First, Laughing Man got knocked flat on his backside, then Mr. Tall got pushed back against the wall. Mr. Pleasant was managing to trade blows with his orc, but it looked like he might get killed at any moment.

Mr. Priest moved up, trying to block an orc's blow with his short staff.

No good. He's being overpowered.

Choco and Ms. Short Hair were holding each other tight and cowering.

What are they doing? That's like asking them to kill you.

Of course, the orcs wouldn't pass up that chance.

He wanted to help, but—Haruhiro couldn't possibly make it in time.

"Ohm, rel, ect, palam, darsh...!"

It was Shihoru.

An elemental that looked like a ball of black seaweed fired forth from the tip of Shihoru's staff. The shadow elemental flew in a spiral, striking an orc in the face just as it was about to brutalize Choco and Ms. Short Hair.

It was Shadow Complex.

The shadow elemental splattered on impact, working its way in through the orc's nose and mouth and quickly taking effect. The orc suddenly stood there, staring vacantly. It was a spell that was easy to resist if you were anticipating it, but not as easy as Sleepy Shadow. The orc hadn't seen it coming at all, so the spell had worked well. First, the orc stood there in a vacant stupor. Soon, it'd go into a state of confusion and excitement, losing the ability to make rational decisions.

"Anger...!" Before it could get to that stage, Ranta leapt in and skewered the orc's gullet.

Haruhiro had wanted to be the one to take down that orc, but Ranta had beat him to the punch.

Oh, well. Not much I can do about it.

Haruhiro got behind the orc that had Mr. Tall pushed back against the wall. He threw away his shield.

He really couldn't see that line.

They weren't like the orcs in the camps. The back plate on the red armor that these Zesh Clan orcs wore had no weak points. It was plate mail. His dagger wouldn't go through that. Backstab wasn't going to be good enough.

Haruhiro pinioned the orc, jabbing his dagger into the gap between the orc's helmet and armor. Once he stabbed through its throat and jumped away, Mr. Tall hit the staggering orc with his longsword. He had a reasonable height advantage, so when he swung his longsword down from overhead, it was pretty powerful. Until the orc fell to the ground motionless, Mr. Tall kept on swinging his longsword down at him.

"...Th-thanks," Mr. Tall said breathlessly at last.

Ignoring that, Haruhiro looked around the area. Choco had another orc after her.

"Choco, behind you!" he shouted.

"...!"

She reacted just in the nick of time. Choco jumped to the side, dodging the orc's slash.

"Gashwarl!" the orc roared.

The orc turned his way. It was charging at Haruhiro. A straight-up fight was out of the question. Haruhiro wouldn't stand a chance in one.

Sharpening his senses and mustering them, he focused on the orc's movements.

The weapon. That single-edged sword. I think it's called a gahari. It's coming. From the top left. Knock it back. Swat. Wrist back in position, the next strike is coming from the top right. Swat. Swat. Swat. Swat.

He sure is strong. He's got power. He's not letting up. If anything goes the slightest bit wrong, I'm done for.

If the enemy had made it a test of endurance, relentlessly pushing Haruhiro with safe attacks, he probably would've made a mistake eventually. Thankfully, his opponent went in for the kill, which saved him.

Next, it'll be a big swing. I can't stop that.

Haruhiro took a risk and moved up. He stepped in on the diagonal and, rather than block the gahari with his dagger, he slid his dagger along the gahari's blade. He turned the blow aside.

At the same time, he grabbed the orc's arm. After two days of Barbara-sensei using this technique on him, he'd received two full days of practical combat training with it. He followed up his Swat with an Arrest.

This won't break.

I mean, seriously, orcs have some thick arms.

Making a snap decision, he tried to sweep the orc's leg out from under it while still pushing its elbow joint as far as it would go.

The orc responded. Haruhiro didn't manage to trip it; the orc jumped on its own.

It rolled, then started to get back up. As it did...

"Thanks...!"

There was Moguzo.

Rushing in, Moguzo landed his most deadly attack, the Thanks Slash, on the orc's head. It had been deadly, all right. The orc's head split in two, helmet and all.

Damn, Moguzo's awesome.

"Th-thanks," Choco stammered, her big eyes open wide as she was clutching her chest. She seemed half-stunned.

"Nah—" Haruhiro began to respond, then grabbed Choco by the arm.

It was an orc. Another orc had come.

Moguzo took it on for them, so they were safe for now, but—though he hadn't intended to, Haruhiro noticed he was holding Choco tight to him. He immediately let go and pushed her away.

"S-sorry."

"...No. Hiro, you saved me."

"Well, yeah, but—Ah! Later...!"

Later, what? Haruhiro didn't really know that himself, but right now, he was busy.

"Gahaha! Moguzo's already taken down two of them, huh! That's my partner for you!" Ranta bellowed.

Ranta was using Exhaust to take on one of the orcs. Moguzo kept on swinging hard, looking like he was going to take down yet another.

Shihoru took aim at a distant orc, using her magic to keep him in check. It was reassuring to see Merry there guarding Shihoru.

Haruhiro traded glances with Yume. They'd do their usual routine. Support Moguzo and Ranta in order to deal with the enemies as quickly as possible.

"Haruhiro!" Ranta shouted, leaping back with Exhaust. "What's your relationship with the girl...?"

"Why're you acting like you can afford to ask questions right now?!" Haruhiro screamed.

"I'm acting like I can afford to because I can, duh! Whoa...?!"

"You can't afford to at all!" Haruhiro shouted.

"Shut up, moron! Take that! Reject...!"

When Ranta locked blades with the orc, he tried to push it back, but he wasn't able to put much distance between them.

At some point, Moguzo had ended up fighting two-versus-one. Even though it'd been one-on-one just a moment ago.

Yume was trying to pull one of the orcs away from Moguzo, but that was dangerous in its own way. Haruhiro felt like they'd probably be better off if he bought time against the orc by using Swat.

When he looked over to Shihoru, Merry was swinging her priest's staff to keep an orc away. He needed to do something about that, too.

We're stretched to our limits, he thought. *Still, don't panic. We're not alone. There're other volunteer soldiers here, too. We don't need to be able to defeat them. We just have to slow them down.*

Still, they're not easy enemies. It's taking everything I have just to keep calm. They're scary. For now, deal with Shihoru and Merry. After that... After that... No, don't worry about after that. First—

"Eryeeeeeeeeeeeeeeeeeeeeeeeeeeeeeeeeeeee...!"

What was that voice?

It wasn't an orc. It was a human. The ear-splitting shriek of a woman.

"They're here!" Bri-chan shouted, leaping for joy up on the wall.

The orcs from the north side slowed noticeably. Actually, they were losing their heads. Behind them. That cry had come from behind them.

"They're here! Our reinforcements!" Bri-chan cried, blowing a kiss. "It's Wild Eagle Force! I love you, Kajiko!"

Grimgar of Fantasy and Ash

13. Our Mistake

From there, the fight became one-sided.

Caught in between Haruhiro and the others in the intercepting group from Green Storm Force and Wild Eagle Force, the orcs from the northern side dropped like flies.

How many minutes did it take to eliminate them? It was fast. In mere minutes, more than twenty orcs were transformed into silent corpses.

They were his enemies, so Haruhiro didn't feel sorry for them, but he did think it was kind of brutal. He'd grown used to the smell of death, but when there were this many corpses, it was still pretty hard on him.

Kajiko's Wild Angels walked past Haruhiro's party.

The feathered stoles around their necks, their helmets, and hats, even the feathers on their bandanas...all of them were dyed red with the blood of their enemies.

"...A-awesome...!"

Ranta's staring in admiration, but...that's not awesome, it's scary,

Haruhiro thought.

"Britney! What about the main gate?!" Kajiko asked in a menacing voice, but Bri-chan, who was still up on the east wall, simply shook his head.

"It's no good! It doesn't look like they've broken it! I can't see from here, but it looks like they're fighting a hard battle!"

"In that case, we'll just have to take the keep ourselves!" Kajiko said, spreading her arms wide. "Listen up, volunteer soldiers! The Frontier Army has put one hundred gold coins on the keeper, Zoran Zesh! Also, there are fifty gold coins on the head of Abael, a sorcerer who's killed many soldiers and volunteers with his black magic!"

"One hundred...!"

"A hundred coins!"

"A hundred gold coins!"

"Fifty coins?!"

"One hundred gold?!"

"Did she say one hundred gold?!"

"That's incredible!"

"Seriously...?!"

As if trying to pour cold water on Green Storm Force and Wild Eagle Force as they buzzed with excitement, arrows rained down from the watchtowers. It looked like a number of volunteer soldiers had been hit by them. Laughing Man from Choco's party had an arrow sticking out of his shoulder, and Mr. Priest had started to treat it.

"Sh-shields...!" Haruhiro hastily picked up an orcish shield. However, it looked like nobody was worrying about the arrows much anymore. The volunteer soldiers had a different look in their eyes now.

They wanted to get up the keep stairs. Then from the stairs to inside the keep. There were one hundred gold coins, then fifty more. One hundred. Fifty. One hundred. Fifty.

One hundred and fifty gold total. Was that the only thing in their minds now? Sure, one hundred and fifty gold was a tempting sum. It was so much money that it hardly felt real, but still.

Haruhiro heard a familiar war cry echo through the courtyard.

It was Ron. "Get into that keep! We're gonna be the first ones in!"

While he'd been watching from the stairs on the eastern wall earlier, they'd been being pushed back as often as they'd advanced, but finally, the enemy's tough defense had been broken.

Green Storm Force and Wild Eagle Force were jumbled together, rushing up the outside stairs. It was like a flood of volunteer soldiers. Arrows were raining down from the watchtowers, but there was no stopping this flow.

The wills of individuals in it no longer mattered. None of them could stop. Haruhiro was being pushed along, as well. His comrades were at his side. That much, he could still tell somehow.

"I'm going to the front gate!" Bri-chan shouted. "I'll go check on the main force! Kajiko, I'm counting on you!"

"Britney, by the time you get back, it's all going to be over...!"

"Don't get them worked up! Show some restraint! You're not a bunch of children, you know!"

"You go tell the worthless regular army that I'm going to take that bounty!"

"Honestly...! Don't be reckless, now!"

Is Bri-chan going somewhere? Haruhiro wondered. *He said something about the main gate. I guess it's fine. Whatever. It doesn't matter. I've got bigger worries. It's the outside staircase. Finally, we're on the outside staircase. We're in a real traffic jam here, though.*

Can we go up like this? It's so crowded, I wouldn't think so, but we're moving. Why are we moving so fast? That took no time. We're already on the keep's roof.

Whoa. Who-oa. Wow. The arrows. They're coming at us from three watchtowers. There are arrows coming from three directions. Now this is a real rain of arrows. It's like a downpour.

Haruhiro managed to get his shield up, somehow. In the time it took to reach the keep's entrance, several arrows thudded into his shield.

Just before being pushed through the entrance to the keep, he threw away his shield.

Moguzo. There. Ranta. There. Yume. Shihoru. Merry. There.

He could see Choco's face, too. At least, he thought he could. They were packed in so tight, it was hard to tell. He didn't really have a sense for the inside of the keep, either. For now, he had to go with the flow.

He ran through a corridor, then went down some stairs. From the third floor, to the second, then the first.

The first floor of the keep had a high ceiling. It was wide, too. So wide that it felt like the whole floor was just one open area.

There were staircases in the four corners, with the one Haruhiro and the others came down probably being in the southeast. If he recalled, they'd have to go up the stairs from the first floor to reach the watchtowers. That meant the other three sets of stairs, in the northwest, southwest, and northeast, should lead to the watchtowers.

There were also four doors on the walls, all of them open. Had they already been searched, then? He'd stepped on or jumped over plenty of orc corpses in the corridor, but that was nothing compared to this first floor. In the time it took Haruhiro and the others to get here, a fierce battle must have been fought.

There were ten—no, more than that—dead orcs, as well as a number of fallen volunteer soldiers. Some were being treated by their comrades, while some others weren't. In other words, they were dead.

"Now then, which way's the jackpot?" Kajiko called.

Kajiko and her Wild Angels looked ready to assault the northwest watchtower. Team Renji had chosen the southwest watchtower. Having seen that, most of the other volunteer soldiers were gravitating towards the northeast watchtower.

"What're we gonna do?!" Ranta lifted his helmet's visor, looking from one set of stairs to another. "I doubt we can compete with Kajiko or Renji and win, so should we go for the northeast tower like the others...?"

"Nah—" Haruhiro began.

I need to decide.

Before he could start overthinking things, Haruhiro made his decision. He went on something like a hunch. "Let's go with Renji and his group."

"Are you stupid?! If we go to the same place as those guys, there isn't a chance in hell that we'll be able to take one of the leaders' heads, and you know it!" Ranta shouted.

"Yume and everyone wouldn't be able to take their heads anyway, y'know."

"You idiot! Stupid Yume! You've got to aim higher!" Ranta bellowed.

Shihoru cracked up laughing. "I don't think anyone who believes that if we went with Renji and his group, there's no way we could take one of the leaders' heads has any right to say that..."

"Yeah. Well, sorta. I guess you're right. All right! Plundering it is, then!" Ranta declared.

"Hahaha..." Moguzo laughed.

"What a coward," Merry said coldly.

"And I'm fine with that!" Ranta said with a grin. "For a Dread Knight, those words are the highest of compliments! Mwahahaha! O Darkness, O Lord of Vice, Demon Call!"

From behind Ranta's head, slightly above it, something like a blackish purple cloud appeared. The clouds whirled into a vortex, rapidly taking shape.

It was like a headless torso, with two holes for eyes on its chest and a slit-like mouth beneath. It was a dread knight's familiar, a demon.

"...*Kehe...Kehehehehe...Kehehehe...Kehehehehehehe...Kehe...* Ranta dies."

"Not 'die, Ranta,' but 'Ranta dies'?! You're suddenly predicting my death, Zodiac-kun?!"

"...*Ehehe...* Kill Ranta."

"And now you're uttering death threats?!" Ranta shouted.

"Zodiac-kun, paw!" Yume called, putting out her hand.

Zodiac-kun said "...Die... Ugly..." but still put his hand in hers.

"Ohh!" Yume cried. "Zodiac-kun's such a good boy. But, y'know, callin' people ugly is mean..."

"...*Kehehe...* Sorry..."

"You're all meek now?!" Ranta exclaimed.

Ranta's comedic jab got no reaction from Zodiac-kun. Why did even his own demon torment him?

Choco's party seemed torn on what to do, too.

"You may not appreciate the advice, but you guys shouldn't push yourselves!" Haruhiro told them.

It wasn't clear whether they'd taken Haruhiro's advice or not, but regardless, Choco and her group seemed like they'd be staying on the first floor. There were other parties that were making no attempt to move, too. They were safe this way. It was a good choice.

In truth, Haruhiro and his party might've been better off staying on the first floor, too. Why weren't they doing that? Because they had killed orcs. Having lost their virginity, were they letting it go to their heads? Did they feel like they could take orcs now?

Haruhiro didn't think that was the case. Normally, he would've at least hesitated here. So why had he made his decision immediately?

Was it because he'd felt like it wouldn't be that dangerous if they were with Renji and his group? That was probably part of it. He couldn't deny it.

Team Renji were strong. If he stayed hiding behind Renji, he probably wasn't going to die that easily.

That said, he had no intention of just hiding. Haruhiro knew his party should be able to help, at least, and he intended for them to.

It was strange to say, but Haruhiro felt, at least somewhat, like he wanted to help Renji. Nothing they did would be the deciding factor in the battle, but it wasn't like they wouldn't be able to contribute anything by being there, either. If they were going to go help someone, he'd rather it be Renji. Even though they'd just be seen as unwanted help, or even treated as an outright hindrance. He didn't want to think that they couldn't do anything.

If Haruhiro had been alone, he wouldn't have minded being seen as a good-for-nothing. If they'd mocked him, he would've been able to laugh it off. He could give up on himself. However, he was in a party. He had comrades.

Moguzo was a pretty amazing warrior. Even Ranta, annoying as he was, had tenacity, and there was something unique about the way he used his skills. Yume was always easygoing, so she was easy to get along with, and Shihoru might look plain, but she was always thinking about her comrades, and she could look at the big picture. Merry was working hard to support everyone, too.

Manato. We've shaped up into a good party.

Though it's really unfortunate that you can't be here with us.

I want to take this party as high as it can go.

I don't think there's any need to rush, but even at this stage, I think we can go a little higher.

"Let's goooooooooo....!" Ranta called.

With Ranta taking point, Haruhiro and the others chased after Team Renji. Maybe because they didn't want to compete with Team Renji, not many volunteer soldiers were heading towards the southwest watchtower.

Team Renji climbed the stairs. They raced up them.

"Yume's eyes're spinnin' round and round!" Yume called, laughing.

They could hear noises from above. The sound of battle.

"Did we hit the jackpot?!" someone shouted.

There were volunteer soldiers bunched up near the very top of the stairs.

Five of them. A party, huh? Haruhiro thought.

"What're you doing?!" Ranta bellowed.

A volunteer soldier who looked like a warrior's eyes went wide.

"Even if we wanted to go, we can't—it's gotten really crazy in there!"

"Are you stupid?! If it's gotten crazy in there, that's all the more reason we've got to go in!" Ranta shouted, pushing Zodiac-kun forward. "—Go, Zodiac-kun! Go forth, and come back to tell us what's happening!"

"...Nnnnnn... No, no, no, no, no, no, no... *Kehehehehehehehe...*"

"Why not?!" Ranta screamed.

Haruhiro clicked his tongue. "Forget it! I'll go look! Don't you feel bad for Zodiac-kun?"

"Oh, shove it! Zodiac-kun's mine, so I can do whatever I want with him!"

"...Wh...who're you saying is yours...? I'm not yours... Are you stupid...? Die..."

"If I die, you'll vanish, too! Are you fine with that?!" Ranta shouted.

"...*Eehehehe...* If you'll die...I... I-I-I couldn't be happier... *Ehehehehehe...*"

"Wha—"

Pushing aside a speechless Ranta and passing between the volunteer soldiers who were ahead of them, Haruhiro poked his head out from the stairs.

"Whoa!"

They were serious.

This really is crazy.

The round room at the top of the watchtower was wider than he'd expected, with a ceiling that wasn't low. At a glance, there were more than ten orcs. In the center of the room were Renji and Ron, who were raising hell and seemed to be putting up a good fight, but Chibi-chan, Sassa, and Adachi had been chased to the edge of the room.

Chibi-chan was waving her staff around, somehow managing to protect Sassa and Adachi. The members of Team Renji were the only volunteer soldiers there, and there was only one orc down at this point.

Haruhiro ducked his head back into the stairwell. "This is bad, guys. At this rate, I don't know about Renji and Ron, but Chibi-chan and the others..."

They had to save them.

Could they do it? Them?

It was presumptuous to the point of absurdity to think that they could. Still, Team Renji was in serious trouble. Currently, it was five-on-ten. Team Renji might be strong, but they weren't superhuman. Their opponents weren't weak, either. Actually, they were strong. However, if Haruhiro's party of six joined in, they could turn things around numerically at least.

First, they'd help Chibi-chan's group. Renji and Ron didn't need it. They could handle themselves. Besides, if Haruhiro and the others helped Chibi-chan and her group, it'd make it easier on Renji and Ron, too.

"Moguzo, go up and head to the right!" Haruhiro called. "Chibi-chan and the others are there, so protect them! Ranta and I will go, too! Yume, Shihoru, Merry, keep an eye on the situation and decide for yourselves!"

"Mmhm!" Moguzo said.

"Yeesh, they're so needy..." Ranta muttered.

"Ranta, man, just try telling Renji that to his face!" Haruhiro shot back.

"I can't and you know it! You damn fool!"

"*You're* the damn fool! Let's go!"

Haruhiro, Moguzo and Ranta went up in that order.

He saw it.

The faintly shining line of light.

From the moment he thought he saw it, Haruhiro's body was already in motion, following the line, neither walking nor running. He advanced as if sliding across the floor.

There was no sound.

It wasn't as if everything had stopped, but it all moved at a very gentle pace.

That orc was about to take a swing at Sassa.

Right here.

Backstab.

Even though it was through armor, Haruhiro's dagger slid in smoothly.

It touched something. A vital point.

When he pulled out, the orc crumpled without uttering a noise.

"...What was that?" Sassa seemed dumbfounded.

Haruhiro shook his head in response. Even if she asked, he couldn't explain it well.

"Thanks...!" bellowed Moguzo, using his Thanks Slash to blow away an orc that was about to attack Chibi-chan. "H-hey, you! Zodiac-kun! Help out, would ya! You're not being fair...!"

"...*Hehehehehehehehehehe*... Nnnnnnn... No... You wimpy, wooly caterpillar... Die..."

"Dammit...! There's not quite enough space, so this is hard!"

Ranta was running around to avoid a direct exchange of blows. Still, he was handling an orc by himself, so he wasn't doing too badly.

Yume, Shihoru and Merry came up, too.

"Renji!" Haruhiro used Swat on an orc's slash, then backed away, leaving the next attack to Sassa.

Sassa was good at using Swat. Haruhiro must've had considerably more muscle strength than her, but Sassa was flexible and moved with comfort. She had a sense of rhythm.

Haruhiro shouted out, "Chibi-chan and the others are fine!"

Renji glanced over at Haruhiro, smiling faintly.

Ahh.

He really is amazing.

Renji used his entire body to make Ish Dogran's sword spin around. It almost looked like he was dancing. What kind of technique was that? Was it a skill?

Slice, slice—Renji laid two orcs low, one after another. Ron took one out as well, cutting it down with all his might. Then Renji took out yet another, decapitating the orc this time.

"Zeel, mare, gram, fel, kanon."

Adachi used the spell Freezing Blood to freeze an orc's feet. Despite that, the orc still continued to stumble along.

"Zeel, mare, gram, terra, kanon." Without missing a beat, Adachi began chanting his next spell.

It was Ice Globe. The ice elemental instantaneously froze the water in the atmosphere. The resultant sphere of ice smashed beautifully into the orc's face.

It looked painful. The orc dropped to his knees.

Without a moment's delay, Sassa moved up.

She went past the orc. Immediately after, Sassa buried her dagger in the orc's neck.

So, you can pull off a Backstab like that, too? Haruhiro thought.

What a combo. Well, we aren't doing bad, ourselves.

"Ohm, rel, ect, nemun, darsh!" Shihoru stopped an orc with Shadow Bond, Merry gave it a good hard whack with her priest's staff, Yume stabbed it with her machete to make it back off, then—Moguzo.

"Hunghh...!"

He didn't use the Thanks Slash. He stepped in, sticking his arm out straight in a one-handed thrust. It was First Thrust.

The orc's throat was basically pulverized. Of course, that meant its neck was broken. There was no way it'd be getting back up.

Haruhiro looked around the area. Were there any enemies?

None.

The orcs were all collapsed on the ground.

"Dammit..." Ron shook his bloody sword. "We didn't need your help."

"What was that?!" Ranta closed in on Ron assertively, but one glare was all it took to make him shrink back at the speed of light.

"...I-I'm sorry. It won't happen again."

"Wimp..." Merry muttered.

"Wimpy, wimpy, wimpy... *Kehehehehehe*... Wimpy, wooly caterpillar... *Ehehe*... Caterpillar, caterpillar, caterpillar, caterpillar..."

"...An actual caterpillar would be more useful, don't you think?" Shihoru asked.

It doesn't stand out, but Shihoru can be pretty mean, Haruhiro thought. *I agree with her, though.*

"Since caterpillars're cute, y'know," Yume nodded.

That, I can't agree with.

"You helped," Renji said.

Man, even Renji's voice is cool. It's low and husky. It's intimidating, but there's a vague sadness there. When I hear him saying we helped, with that voice—Honestly, it's just overwhelming.

It frustrated him, so Haruhiro tried to feign calmness, shrugging. "We owed you one."

"Now we're even," Renji said.

"...Are we?" Haruhiro asked.

"Yeah," Renji said, looking to Moguzo. "You. I could use you."

"Huh...?" Moguzo's eyes darted around rapidly, then he pointed to himself. "Whaaa?! Y-y-y-y-you mean me...?! N-no, that's not...uh, I-I'm not that impressive..."

What did Renji mean, he could "use" him? That may have bothered Haruhiro a little, but both Renji and Moguzo were warriors. "It takes a warrior to know one"—he didn't know if there was an expression like that, but a warrior had to know a lot about what it meant to be one. What was more, he was being recognized by Renji, the guy who had the attention of more volunteer soldiers than anyone else. Moguzo had to be proud of that.

Moguzo really is amazing, Haruhiro thought. *Our Moguzo is amazing.*

"Regardless," Adachi said, adjusting the position of his glasses, taking on a calm and sarcastic tone, "it seems the prize isn't here. Should you be taking it easy now, Renji?"

Renji didn't respond. In place of a response, he turned towards the stairs. That was when it happened.

"Hey! Below!" someone said.

Someone. Not from Team Renji or Haruhiro's party. Not here.

Haruhiro twisted his head. "Below...?"

Renji took off at a run.

"Haruhiro!" Ranta slapped Haruhiro on the back. "We're going, too!"

What could it be? Weird. My heart. It's pounding like crazy. Below. What's happening below? Below. Wait, below...?

They descended the spiral staircase.

It felt like his ears were plugged. Strange. Why? Why was he so shaken? He didn't understand. What was the reason? The cause? Haruhiro had lost his head to the point where he couldn't make sense of anything.

He was unsteady on his feet.

Even so, his body had to keep moving.

Downwards.

To the first floor.

They were dead.

Volunteer soldiers.

So many of them.

There was a large number of corpses.

There were orcs. Why? Where had these guys come from? It was more than just one or two. There were a ton of them.

In the middle, there was one orc bigger than all the others. The orc wore a deep, venomously deep, red suit of armor and helm, with hair dyed black and gold spilling out from underneath it. What was more, he used a two-sword style. He was built incredibly tough, carrying two scimitars that screamed danger, one in each hand, of course.

Zoran.

Zoran Zesh.

There was no doubt about it. He matched every distinguishing trait Bri-chan had told them. This was Keeper Zoran, the head of the

Zesh Clan, who had a one hundred gold coin bounty on his head.

Zoran was using his scimitars to cut people down.

That's Mr. Pleasant, Haruhiro realized, recognizing one of them. From Choco's party.

Mr. Pleasant might've been trying to block Zoran's scimitar with his sword. However, he didn't make it in time.

"Ahh!" Mr. Pleasant let out a scream that sounded a little stupid. Both his arms were severed at the same time.

Then, without any delay, his head.

Mr. Pleasant's head went flying.

It happened so easily.

What is this?

What's going on?

Where's Laughing Man? Mr. Priest? Ms. Short Hair, the mage? *They're not here.*

No, there they were.

They had fallen.

All of them, chopped to pieces.

Mr. Tall was just barely holding on, fighting with his back to the wall against an orc who wasn't Zoran. Next to him, Choco.

Choco was here.

Mr. Tall was trying to protect Choco. However, he was clearly taking a beating, and he couldn't fully protect her.

Strong. Those orcs were strong. They were nothing like the orcs they'd gone against so far.

It wasn't their equipment—it was something about the way they were built, or even the air about them. They were totally different. These were the keeper and his close associates.

There were a number of unarmored orcs with pots of some sort hanging from their hips that looked like mages. No, not mages—they were called sorcerers, right?

Team Renji was already attacking the orcs. However, there were more than ten of them, probably around twenty, and the first floor was wide and open. Needlessly so.

How were Mr. Tall and Choco?

"Urkh!" Mr. Tall had locked blades with one of the keeper's associates, but he must've been kicked in the belly or something, because he'd doubled over.

Hey.

No.

You can't do that.

You can't be doing that.

Choco had her dagger in a fighting stance. With both hands on the hilt, she had the blade pointed towards the orc.

The blade's tip quivered. She was terrified.

No. That isn't going to be good enough.

"Choco!" Haruhiro screamed, starting to run.

In that moment, it felt like Choco looked at him. Probably, she did try to look.

The orc's sword sank into Choco's shoulder. It went in really deep.

The orc kicked her to the ground, tearing his sword free and immediately swinging it down at her.

"Sto—"

Once.

Twice.

Three times, the orc swung his sword down.

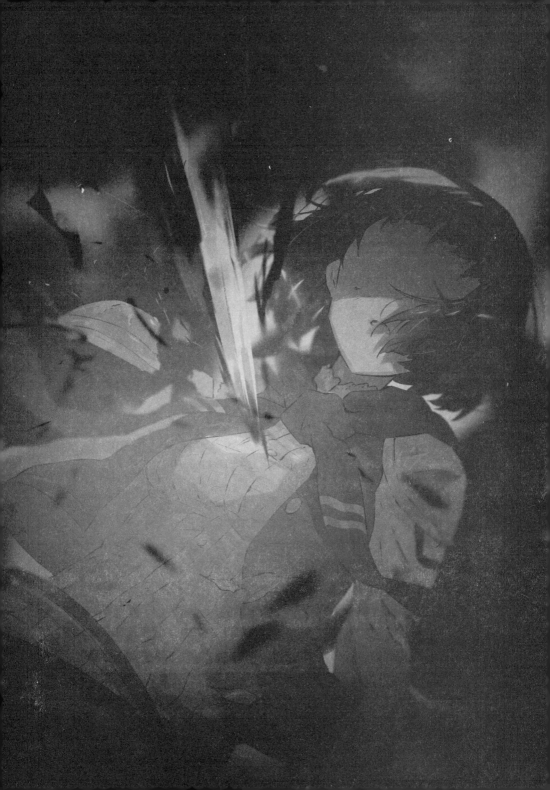

Choco.

Ahh!

Choco.

How? Why? This can't...

No.

Haruhiro clutched his head. A voice came out on its own. He didn't know what was going on, he really didn't know himself what the voice was. He didn't know.

What the hell was this?

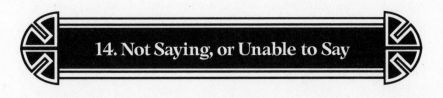

14. Not Saying, or Unable to Say

That vending machine was right next to my house. It was really just a minute or two's walk away, and if I walked a bit further, there was a convenience store, too, but no matter what time of the day it was, if I went that far, I'd run into people I knew, and I kind of didn't want to, so that vending machine was like my refuge... I mean, I say refuge, but it's not like I really wanted to run away, or wanted to escape, not all the time, it's just, well, when I kinda wanted to run away, sort of, like I couldn't take it anymore, I'd get out of the house and kill time near that vending machine.

When did I start doing it?

Was it in elementary school?

Well, around fifth grade or so? Maybe.

I didn't have a room to myself, and my older brother was always there, and I couldn't relax, so I wanted to be alone, I guess. Though, if I said that, I'm sure my brother would tell me not to be a cheeky brat, and he'd kick me, but, yeah, I'm sure there were times I wanted to be alone.

So, I'd go to the vending machine and buy juice, or not buy juice, and drink it, or not drink it.

As I was staring off into space, I'd start to feel like maybe it was time to head home, and then I'd just sort of do it.

That was what it was like at first, but one time, when I was in sixth grade, it was hot outside, it was summer, I think, and when I went to where the vending machine was, someone came along and I thought maybe I should hide, but that felt kind of awkward, so I thought maybe I'd just pretend not to notice them, but it was someone I knew, Choco, who lived nearby.

Choco had her hair cut like a kappa. A bob cut, I think it's called. Like, seriously, she'd had it like that ever since she was little, and if I ever looked up bobbed hair, I wouldn't be surprised to find a picture of Choco, that's how strong the connection between the two was.

She wasn't sociable at all, and you could never tell quite what she was thinking. At school and places like that, she was the type who always seemed a little bit out of place. But, well, only a little bit.

It wasn't like she had no friends, or anything like that. But rather than being really close friends with anyone, she just hung out with a group of people, sort of.

I dunno why, but from the time we were in preschool, I'd been interested in Choco. Like, "Y'know, there's something kind of different about her." To be honest, I just couldn't get her out of my head, because, well, I guess you could say I loved her.

Actually, Choco was the first person I'd ever fallen in love with, and I'd been in love with her ever since. I mean, we'd been together since preschool, after all, and we'd been in the same class a number of times, and our houses were close, and we talked, too, because we were pretty close, but I'd never confessed my love to her, or anything like that.

Well, it wasn't like I could have.

I think it happened in third grade. There were rumors going around that Choco liked Kawabe-kun, and when we were alone together after school, I asked her if they were true, just like that, as subtly as I could, and she thought for a little while and then answered, "Yeah..."

That. That was a shock.

A pretty major one.

Kawabe-kun was slender, not really athletic or anything, but he was learning piano. He came from, I guess you could say, a good upbringing...

Ah, so that's what Choco's into, I thought. *I see.*

So that's it.

Is that it?

Nah, it can't be, I thought.

Kawabe-kun had all these things I didn't, but, actually, once in a while, we'd play together, and Kawabe-kun was a really good guy. I had no complaints about him. He was pretty high up on my friends list, you could say, and I had a good impression of him, so it was like, "Oh, Choco likes Kawabe-kun, huh..."

Like, "Well, Kawabe-kun is a good guy, after all."

Like, "You know, I don't really know what to do, but I've gotta be supportive."

I mean, it'd have been awkward if she'd fallen for some weirdo, but this was Kawabe-kun. Kawabe-kun was a good guy.

That was what I thought, so I made a suggestion. "Hey, Choco, why don't you give him, like, a letter, or something? Kawabe-kun, his house is pretty strict, so he doesn't have a cellphone, but a letter, yeah, I think Kawabe-kun would read it. I think he'd give you a response, too. I mean, it's Kawabe-kun. How about it?"

Choco said she didn't need to. That she was fine without it. She had no intention of doing anything like that.

Oh, okay. I see. Hmm.

She just liked him. That was all.

That was Choco's answer. She just liked him.

Still, you know, I tried a lot of things. Like finding ways for Choco to talk to Kawabe-kun as much as possible. Or setting it up so Choco and Kawabe-kun could be alone together. When I look back at it now, it was all pretty blatant and awkward, but I was frantically doing everything I could back then. I mean, Kawabe-kun, he was a good guy, and Choco... I loved Choco.

Anyway, during the summer that I was in sixth grade, Choco came to the vending machine, and when she called out to me to ask what I was doing, I answered, "Oh, nothing, I'm just sorta hanging out here," and Choco, she was feeling hot, so she wanted a cold can of soda, but there weren't any in the refrigerator at her house, so she'd come here to buy one, so, well, we talked there for, like, ten, fifteen minutes, and after that, when I'd go to the vending machine, sometimes Choco would be there.

Choco would buy a cold soda, or, when it was cold, a warm can of corn potage.

Choco would complain that soda bothered her throat, but then drink it anyway, or call corn potage "conpotage," or say "Hot, hot," and blow on it to cool it down, and I really did love her for all of that, but, I dunno, it wasn't that I loved her so much it was unbearable, it was a natural love, you know, it was just there, like the air, like, "Well, yeah, of course I love her," and it'd always been like that.

Choco was the type to fall for boys pretty often. She didn't let it show, though.

According to her, she'd just vaguely start thinking, "Hey, he's nice," and then she'd find herself thinking about that guy all the time, so then she'd realize, "I'm in love, huh," and as long as she could keep thinking that, she'd stay in love.

Didn't she want to go out with them?

When I asked her that, she answered that she wasn't completely uninterested in that, but that she didn't feel strongly about it. I guess that was just how it was.

Since I loved Choco, I did think I'd want to go out with her if I could, but Choco was in love with someone, some other guy, and when I couldn't help but ask her who it was that she liked now, she'd always tell me honestly. Then I'd think, "Well, you know, even if she doesn't intend to do anything about it, I hope they can be friends, or that they can get to know each other better..." and somehow, I'd end up trying to make that happen.

Even though Choco never asked me to, I did it on my own.

It's not that I didn't think, "Why am I even doing this?"

I mean, I thought that a lot. And that I was being an idiot, too.

Choco was unsociable, and she was kind of expressionless, but when she was talking to a guy she liked, she'd get excited, and when they were done talking, she'd stare off into space, or her face would turn a little red.

When I thought "Ah, Choco's happy," it made me happy, too.

I don't know how to say it, but even though I'd known Choco a long time, think about it as hard as I might, I didn't really know how to make Choco happy.

Choco was pretty mysterious. She didn't read, she didn't listen to music, she barely watched TV, and when, once in a while, she found something like a hobby, she tired of it in no time.

When I asked her, "Is there nothing you really, really like?" she immediately responded, "Yeah, there's nothing."

She was hard to grasp, which was why she interested me, and I wanted to make her happy, wanted to see her smile, but I just couldn't figure out how.

That was what Choco was like.

So, no matter what it took, I wanted to make Choco happy.

Though, yeah, it was a little painful.

That night, too, as I was sitting in front of the vending machine, Choco came along.

I kinda had a vague feeling she would, but often, when I got that feeling, she wouldn't end up coming. But that night, Choco actually came, and, in my mind, I wanted to shout out "Yes!" and pump my arm, but I held back.

With feigned calmness, I greeted her with a "Yo," and Choco raised her right hand in response, saying, "Yo" back.

The way she spoke and her little gestures, they were super adorable, and I thought, "Yeah, that's it," reaffirming that I loved Choco, but right then Choco loved this guy in our class who had an uncommon name, Hidemasa... This Hidemasa, he was a good guy, and he looked good, too, so I thought Choco had good taste in guys.

How should I put it?

He was one of those guys who weren't super popular with the girls or anything, but when you looked at them as another guy, you thought, "But he's a good guy, you know? Why don't girls see that?" But no, they did see it, and there was always one, or two, or maybe a few girls who were secretly crushing on them. That type. Choco always fell for guys like that.

Like, "Yeah, even I can totally see why."

Like, "Well, if it's him, I can't complain."

Of course, I'd want to support her, and I did. I mean, I was no match for guys like that. I'd start getting ahead of myself, thinking things like, "He could make Choco happy."

Choco bought herself a soda. One of those lemon-lime drinks. She opened it with the pull-tab, then took a sip. She grimaced just a little, letting out a groan.

"My throat hurts."

"Hey," I said.

"Hm?"

"If it hurts, why drink soda?" I asked.

"Because I want to drink it."

"Of course."

"But, you know, drinking it too often is probably bad for my health," she added.

"Could be. Athletes aren't supposed to drink it, I hear. Soda."

"Oh, I see," she said. "Not that I'm athletic at all."

"Well, maybe it's okay, then," I said.

"It's only once in a while."

"You say that, but don't you drink it pretty often?" I asked.

"I only really drink it here," she said.

"I see."

I tried telling her about how I'd gone to karaoke with Hidemasa recently. Choco didn't seem interested. She also seemed like she might be feigning disinterest, but listening closely.

I figured that, yeah, she had to be listening, so I told her about the songs Hidemasa sang. Like how it was mostly pop idol songs that were popular a little while ago, and he seemed to be trying to match everyone else's tastes. But since they were songs everyone knew, everyone really got into it.

I talked about how Hidemasa could be like that sometimes. When I was feeling a little exhausted and went quiet, Hidemasa struck up a conversation with me because he was concerned. I talked about what a great guy Hidemasa could be.

"Me," Choco said, speaking up suddenly. "I can't be considerate, and I can't look out for other people, so maybe I like people who can do that."

"Oh," I said. "That makes sense. Like looking to find what you, yourself lack in others?"

"Do you think I lack consideration for others, too, Hiro?" she asked.

"No, that's not it. You don't do things that make people feel uncomfortable, do you?"

"Maybe I don't."

"Yeah, that's what I thought."

"You don't either, Hiro."

I was surprised. "Really? Huh? Am I managing to be considerate?"

"Like you are to me?"

"Hmm. Well, we've known each other a long time, after all."

"Don't you have one, Hiro?" she asked.

"Huh? One what?"

"A person you love, or a girl you're interested in."

I was at a loss for what to say, and I thought hard, my brain racing like crazy, and I did think this might be my big chance to tell her, but then I thought, no, it wasn't my chance, how could it possibly be, and thought better of it.

I love Choco, but it's not quite like that, I thought.

It was like that, but it wasn't.

What was it?

It felt like it'd already gone past that point. Like it had transcended it.

I didn't care about myself, but I was happy as long as Choco was happy. It seemed stupid, and if you asked me whether I really felt that way—I wondered about that.

Things are fine the way they are. That's what I might've been thinking.

If I kept the same distance from her that I always had, we could talk like this sometimes. If Choco got herself a boyfriend someday, that might change, though. If it happened, it happened. That'd be fine in its own way, I felt.

I mean, Choco had always loved someone else, and I'd always watched her, so painful as that would be, I was used to it.

I did love Choco, though.

"I don't," I said. "If I did, I'd tell you."

"Not that I really want to know," she said.

"Wow. You're awful. After all the times I've listened to you talk about yours."

"You weak-willed wussy," she said.

"...Did you say something?"

"Yeah. I said something."

"I heard you..."

I wondered what that insult was supposed to mean.

Though, maybe, Choco might have realized. That I was in love with her.

Would she have been able to figure out that much? She would, huh.

Choco crouched down next to me. Her shoulder was next to mine. Choco was looking downwards.

"Someday, Hiro, if you find a person you love..."

"...Yeah?"

"...Tell me."

"I thought you didn't want to know."

"Not really," she said. "But tell me."

"Well, okay."

Choco turned a little to face me, smiling slightly, her eyes narrowing a little. "Hiro, you don't lie."

"Well, there's a time and place for everything," I said. "But I don't lie to you... I don't think?"

"I know."

I'm lying, though. It's probably blatantly obvious, too.

Listen, I... For a long time now...

For as long as I can remember, I've loved you, and only you.

I can't say it, though.

I'm sure I'll go my whole life without ever sayi—

15. The Line of Death

...I recalled something...I think.

He'd recalled many things. That's what it felt like. But he didn't remember.

He'd reached that place. There was no doubt about that. And yet, he didn't remember anything.

Not now.

For a moment, it'd been different. He'd recalled everything.

But, as for what that "everything" had been, he didn't know.

There was no way he shouldn't know. He'd known what it was. He had a strong sense of that, if nothing else.

There was something left behind.

Right here.

Deep inside his chest.

There'd been something here.

It was gone now.

It'd been gouged out, and now there was only a hole left where it once had been.

If he traced the shape of that hole, he could take a pretty good guess at what that was.

It's Choco.

He'd recalled Choco, then forgotten her. It was something about Choco.

Haruhiro had probably known Choco. They'd been acquaintances. Or friends, or something.

Really, that was all he knew.

There was nothing else left. Not even a hint.

"Haruhiro...!" Ranta was shaking him hard. "Hey, man! What are you spacing out on us for?! At a time like this! You can't afford to be doing that...!"

"I—"

I know.

I know that. I do.

...I know that?

Really?

No, Ranta's right. It's just like he said. What am I letting my mind wander for? Keeper Zoran Zesh, his attendants, and the orcish sorcerers are unleashing their fury on the first floor of the fortress. There are volunteer soldiers dropping left and right. Choco. Ohh. Choco.

Choco and her party died, too. They're dead. Mr. Pleasant, Laughing Man, Mr. Priest, Ms. Short Hair, and even Choco. What about Mr. Tall? He's on the ground over by the wall. He's not unharmed; that much I can tell. He's taken a serious wound. They were all killed. By the orcs.

Choco was killed.

Yes, I'm shocked. But while I do feel some sadness, some sorrow, some pain, it's not that bad.

Somehow, that doesn't sit quite right with me. It's like I'm wondering if this is all right. Of course, I'm shocked. She was a volunteer soldier, like me. My junior. I'd spoken to her before, and I might have known her before I came here. Now she's dead. But that's not it.

It's more, well... I feel like there should be more to it than this.

It should be far worse than this. Choco's dead, yet this is all I feel? Isn't that awful?

Not that I have any basis to think that.

Even if we knew each other, I don't know what our relationship was. We might have just known each other and maybe talked before.

Regardless, now was not the time to dwell on it. Ranta was right. They were in a tense situation.

The surviving volunteer soldiers, including Renji and his group, were fighting a desperate battle against Zoran Zesh and his party. As for Renji himself, he was trading blows with Zoran. He was being pushed hard, too.

No, it was far worse than just that. Renji wasn't even deflecting Zoran's scimitar with his sword.

Can't he do it? Haruhiro wondered.

Renji was dodging. He was desperately dodging. He was covered in blood. He didn't seem to have taken a fatal blow, but he had a lot of cuts on his head.

"Dammit!" Ron shouted, rushing in to aid him.

But Renji yelled, "Don't you dare come over here!" at him. "You'll get in my way! Nobody come near us!"

It probably wasn't because it was a one-on-one duel between men, or anything like that. It was because it was too dangerous.

Zoran's long, fat arms. His thick shoulders and chest. Those movements. And finally, that scimitar. Zoran's probably even more dangerous than Ish Dogran, the one who came and attacked Alterna. It'd only take one hit, I'm sure. If he got one solid hit in, it would be over in an instant.

Even his own attendants must've been afraid of getting hit, because they weren't trying to get closer to Zoran.

As a result, Zoran and Renji were facing each other one-on-one, but there was a battle going on between the orc attendants and sorcerers and the volunteer soldiers, too.

A battle we're losing, Haruhiro thought. *One we're losing badly.*

Ron's locked blades with an orc attendant, but looks like he's having a hard time. Chibi-chan, Sassa, and Adachi have been pushed back up against the wall. How many volunteer soldiers are actually fighting on even footing with the orc attendants? Very few. The rest could go down at any moment, or are going down already.

"Sorcerer!" Shihoru shouted.

Haruhiro looked and saw there was an orc who seemed to be a sorcerer coming in their direction from near the bottom of the stairs.

"Hungahh...!" Moguzo shouted.

When Moguzo moved up, the sorcerer stopped walking and lifted up the pot hanging from his waist, opening the lid on it. Something was coming out of the pot.

Bugs, Haruhiro thought. *Bugs, huh? It's probably bugs. A swarm of bugs.*

"Ow?!" Moguzo cried out in confusion as the bugs swarmed over his head. He was wearing a helmet, but the bugs were tiny. It looked like they were getting in through the opening. "—Gwahhhhhh....!"

Moguzo screamed in agony, looking like he was going to sit down.

That's dangerous, Haruhiro thought. *He can't.*

"Don't sit down!" Haruhiro shouted, reacting immediately. "Moguzo, don't sit down! You can't stop!"

"Hungh!" Moguzo shouted, swinging his sword around unsteadily. "Hwahhhhh...!"

"Damn you and your petty tricks!" Ranta shouted, but as he was running forward, he froze in a bizarre pose.

"...Guh, nghhhhhhh...." Ranta muttered.

"What...?!" Haruhiro gasped. *Could this be sorcery, too?*

The sorcerer who'd unleashed the bugs on Moguzo now had his palm pointing towards Ranta.

"Is it psychokinesis?!" Haruhiro cried.

"Nyeh!" Yume shouted, readying her bow and firing an arrow.

The sorcerer leapt backwards to dodge the arrow, but it looked like Ranta was able to move now.

That's great, but her arrow grazed Ron's face, Haruhiro thought.

"Hey! Watch it!" Ron shouted.

"Wah! S-sorry!" Yume cried.

"You can't use your bow, Yume!" Haruhiro called. "This is a melee!"

"Right, yeah, got it!"

"Ohm, rel, ect, palam, darsh!" Shihoru called.

A shadow elemental fired out of the tip of Shihoru's staff. The shadow elemental flew in a spiral, hitting the sorcerer and then forcing its way into his body through his nose and mouth.

It was Shadow Complex.

Did she get him? Haruhiro wondered.

The sorcerer stumbled for a moment, then shook his head. But that was all.

Shihoru clenched her teeth. "He resisted it!"

"Leave this to me!" Ranta shouted. "Hatred...!"

Ranta took a sharp step towards him, but the sorcerer had seen it coming. He leapt back nimbly, with Orc Attendant A moving up to take his place.

Orc Attendant A's gahari and Ranta's longsword collided.

Their blades locked.

"Hah! Reject!" Ranta immediately pushed him away, trying to put some distance between them, but Orc Attendant A pushed back into him.

"Ooosh...!" the orc grunted.

"Nwah!" Ranta shouted.

Ranta's losing his balance, Haruhiro thought. *This is really bad. He's gonna get taken out. I've gotta support him. Can I do it?* Haruhiro asked himself. *I'm going to do it.*

When Haruhiro tried to leap in, Orc Attendant B moved up and blocked his path.

He's really intimidating, Haruhiro thought. *I'm breaking into a cold sweat. Do I really have to do this? This is nuts.*

"Osh! Osh! Osh! Osh!" the orc called.

"Ah! Ah...! Ah! Ah...!" Haruhiro gasped out.

Swat. Swat. Swat. Swat.

This is bad. My hands are going numb. My eyes are spinning. I'm scared. Way too scared. I can't do this. He's strong. He's got power.

I'm gonna get killed.

"Smash!" Merry's timing was perfect. She whacked Orc Attendant B with her priest's staff.

No, it wasn't good enough, huh? Haruhiro realized.

Orc Attendant B easily knocked her staff back with his shield, and then, with his body still turned towards Haruhiro, he looked towards Merry.

...It was good enough, Haruhiro thought. *Now.*

Haruhiro charged towards Orc Attendant B with all his strength.

Orc Attendant B may have been trying to bash Haruhiro with his shield, but Haruhiro slipped past it.

As he went by, he copied Sassa's trick and rammed his dagger into Orc Attendant B's neck.

I almost had him.

"Gwah...?!" Haruhiro yelped.

Bugs. It's bugs.

Haruhiro immediately closed his mouth, shut his eyes, and lowered his posture.

Bugs. It's bugs. The sorcerer. When? Where was he? Bugs. The bugs.

"Get back, Haru!" a voice yelled.

That's Merry. She's telling me to get back, but where do I back off to? Wait, there are bugs in my mouth. I want to spit them out, but if I open my mouth, I think more will get in. I can't open my eyes, either. What's going on? I have no clue. This is bad. Seriously bad.

I'm gonna die.

There might be an orc trying to kill Haruhiro right now. He could die at any moment.

"Haru-kun, this way!" someone shouted, grabbing him by the arm and pulling.

Yume, huh? he thought.

Suddenly, something occurred to him.

Water. Use water.

Haruhiro pulled out his canteen, pouring its contents all over himself. He rinsed off his face and spat out the bugs.

I can see. I can breathe, too.

"—It's okay now!" Yume called.

No, this is not okay at all, Haruhiro thought. *Ranta's being overwhelmed by Orc Attendant A. He could go down at any moment. Maybe it's because of the bugs, but Moguzo looks like he's just barely managing to handle Orc Attendant B. Merry's putting up a good fight to protect Shihoru from Orc Attendant C, but it's looking dicey. I've gotta do something.*

As for Team Renji, Renji's still being chased around by Zoran, and the other four look like they're stuck on the defensive and just barely holding out.

How many volunteer soldiers are still alive?

Wiped out.

Those words just came to mind.

Like I'd let that happen, Haruhiro thought. *Us getting wiped out. Don't be ridiculous.*

"Yume, look after Merry!" he shouted.

Haruhiro sent Yume over to Merry and decided to help Ranta himself. The problem was, how would he help him? If he tried to get behind Orc Attendant A, he worried another orc would get behind him.

I saw a sword, he thought. *It's on the ground. A sword. Whose is it? Doesn't matter.*

Haruhiro picked up the sword and threw it at Orc Attendant A. It was a desperate move, but Orc Attendant A used his shield to block the incoming sword and backed off slightly. It looked like that had let

Ranta catch his breath for a moment.

"Damn, I can't keep this up...!" Ranta panted. "Seriously! Seriously...!"

"What happened to Zodiac-kun?!" Haruhiro yelled.

"He got taken out!" Ranta shouted. "In one blow! That idiot's weak! Anger...!"

If Ranta was turning to go on the offensive even in this situation, he might be pretty impressive. However, Orc Attendant A was even better. He swept Ranta's longsword aside like it was nothing. Orc Attendant A used his riposte to strike Ranta in the head.

His head, Haruhiro thought. *That was his head.*

"Ow!" Ranta moaned.

Sure, he's wearing a helmet, but the head is dangerous.

Ranta staggered.

"I'm not gonna let you kill him!" Haruhiro charged at Orc Attendant A with reckless abandon—or that was what he made it look like, before falling into a defensive stance when Orc Attendant A turned to face him.

Bring it. Come attack me. Here he comes. Swat, swat, swat.

"Pull yourself back together, Ranta!" he called.

"I don't need you to tell me that! Ohhhhhhhh! One Hundred Rending Slashes of Repentance!"

There's no skill called that, Haruhiro thought. *He's spouting nonsense.*

Ranta was using his longsword to unleash a flurry of blows on Orc Attendant A.

Well, they're all getting blocked, though. Still, Orc Attendant A is going on the defensive.

I know. I'll attack.

Even if it means being a little reckless, I need to attack. I've got to reduce the number of enemies, even if it's just by one, or we're not going to get anywhere.

Behind him. Get behind Orc Attendant A. Take him down with a single Backstab. I'll do it. I'm doing this.

It happened the moment Haruhiro made his decision.

"Myeek!" somebody screamed.

It's Yume, Haruhiro thought. *That scream is Yume. She's fallen to the ground. Or rather, she must have been sent flying.*

She was covered in blood from her shoulder to her breast.

Did she get hit? he thought. *By Orc Attendant C?*

Orc Attendant C went to attack Yume. Merry tried to stand in his way, swinging her priest's staff around, but, cruelly, Orc Attendant C was able to easily deflect it with his shield.

"Oh, crap!" Haruhiro dashed. *I might not make it.*

Yume, however, did everything she could. She tossed a throwing knife. "Star Piercer!"

Orc Attendant C took a step back, dodging the throwing knife.

Even if that only bought a few seconds, it looks like I'll make it in time, Haruhiro thought. *I don't care what happens to me now.*

Haruhiro was planning to grapple Orc Attendant C.

But what's that? he thought. *There's something coming from the side. A presence to my left.*

Despite himself, he looked. It was a good thing he did. It was the sorcerer. He had inhaled deeply, and looked like he was about to spit something.

What is it? Coming out of his mouth— "Fire...!"

Inhaling sharply in surprise, Haruhiro quickly threw himself to the ground.

I just barely managed to avoid taking a fire bath, but it's hot, he thought. *Man, it's hot. Wait, I'm on fire. My cloak is. But before that, Yume.*

It's over.

Orc Attendant C was about to swing his sword down on her.

It was over. Yume was going to get taken out.

No!

"Hungahh...!"

It wasn't over. Moguzo was here. Haruhiro and the others had Moguzo.

Moguzo slammed himself into Orc Attendant C, knocking the orc away. But there was still the sorcerer. The sorcerer was coming again. Using that flamethrower. He spewed flames, turning Moguzo into a ball of fire. The sorcerer ran away, perhaps scared by Moguzo's intensity as he seemed to shrug that off, swinging The Chopper around wildly.

"Retreat!" Haruhiro screamed, thinking that was their only option.

It's too much. We can't win this. We'll die. At this rate, all of us will die. I don't want to die. Not because I'm afraid of death, but because I don't want to let my comrades die. I don't want them to die. They can't. I won't let them die.

"Let's pull back!" he called. "To the watchtower we were in before!"

But...can we do it?

Grimgar
of
Fantasy and Ash

16. Last Stand

To answer that question, yes, they managed it.

Haruhiro remembered pulling off his burning cloak and throwing it over a nearby orc, then pulling Yume to her feet and making her run. Honestly, he didn't remember what happened after that. It was all a blur.

There'd been a party that hadn't gone down to the first floor who'd been staying on the watchtower stairs to wait and see what happened. After taking their places, or forcing them out, Haruhiro and the others were now taking a short rest.

Merry had treated Yume's serious injuries first, and she'd now moved on to treating Moguzo. His armor and helmet were intact, but having taken a direct hit from that flamethrower attack, he must've been burned.

Was he okay? No, there was no way he could be totally okay.

"Thanks, Moguzo," Yume said, sitting down next to Moguzo. "Moguzo, if you hadn't come, Yume thinks she would have died."

"N-nah," Moguzo said. "Uh...but what are comrades for?"

"Oh, yeah," Yume said. "That's right, huh."

Ranta was sitting on the stairs, holding his knees. He was being awfully quiet. Merry wasn't doing much talking, and Shihoru had fallen silent. Haruhiro didn't want to speak, either.

This is bad, he thought.

That was seriously dangerous. It's a wonder that everyone is still alive. A miracle. If we'd made one mistake anywhere—no, we did make mistakes. Lots of them, probably. Then again, regardless of whether we made mistakes or not, if our luck had gone bad, someone would have died. Once one person died, it would all have fallen apart from there. A second and a third would've died, and in no time, we'd have been wiped out. It was luck. We got lucky. That's all.

Retreating.

Even now, he wasn't sure if that'd been the right call. If one of them had gone down while withdrawing, they would've been wiped out, or close to it. It'd been pure chance that that hadn't happened.

It was a good thing it hadn't, but Haruhiro couldn't take credit for that. They'd just gotten lucky.

"...What do we do?" Ranta asked in a whisper.

No one answered. What would they do?

What do we do? Haruhiro thought. *Hold on. It's impossible. We can't fight anymore. We're totally outclassed. Even Renji and his party are struggling. Not just struggling; they were on the verge of going down. They may already have.*

Haruhiro raised his face. When he did, he realized he'd been looking down.

All of his comrades' gazes were focused on him. Why was that?

...Oh, right.

Was it because he was the leader? Because Haruhiro was the leader of this party? Did that mean he had to make a decision about what they were going to do?

Well, even if they ask me, I can't decide that, he thought. *Don't be ridiculous. Don't push this off on me. I don't have the power for that. The responsibility is too heavy. I can't do it, okay? I mean, too many have died. There are a ton of people who've died. It's scary, okay? All of this stuff. Just stop it already. Dying—*

She did die, didn't she, he realized. *Choco died, too.*

Are all of us going to die? Renji, his party, and then us? Everyone?

We'll die, just like Choco.

We can't do it.

It's already over. I want to say that to them, but I can't decide anything. I don't want to anymore. Stop it. I can't take being leader anymore. I don't care. Do whatever you want. You can all do whatever you want. Don't look to me for anything. Don't expect anything. I can't bear that burden. I can't, okay? Well, I guess we're gonna die. We have no choice but to die. There's nothing we can do about it. If you don't like that, then someone else make a decision. Put out some ideas. Say, "Why don't we do this?" Tell me what we can do.

I can't say it.

If he said that, it was plain as day what would happen. The party would fall apart.

Ahh, he realized. *No, It's not like that. It's not.*

That wasn't it.

In the end, this was all about him.

Even in this desperate situation, he wanted to keep up appearances. He wanted to look cool. He didn't want his comrades to give up on him in dismay. Haruhiro wasn't an upstanding leader, and he probably couldn't become one. Still, he didn't want his comrades to think of him as the worst leader ever. He didn't want everyone to hate him. He didn't want to be given up on. Until the very end, he wanted them to think of him as a comrade.

There's a limit to how pathetic I can let myself be, he thought. *Giving up...it doesn't get lamer than that. It's just too awful. But in the end, was this all I could manage? I'm not Manato so, well, I guess it was.*

"...I'll go scope things out," he said.

Haruhiro and his party were huddled together a small distance up the spiral staircase. If they stayed here, they'd continue to hear the sounds of battle and voices, but they wouldn't have a good idea what was going on.

They were probably here because they'd rather not know. No one made any attempt to move.

Haruhiro felt the same. However, it was better than staying here, exposed to everyone's greedy—well, that word would be a bit unkind—clinging gazes that pleaded for him to do something. Besides, it wasn't like he didn't feel morbidly curious.

Haruhiro went down the stairs and poked his head out. He clenched his teeth.

"...Renji."

Team Renji was still fighting hard. Ron and Chibi-chan were bloody from fighting to protect Adachi and Sassa, while Renji's epic duel with Keeper Zoran Zesh was still ongoing. Zoran was hardly scratched, while Renji was in such a state that you couldn't even tell where his injuries were, but he was still on his feet, constantly moving to avoid Zoran's two swords.

Epic. Yes, epic was the only word to describe it.

As for other surviving volunteer soldiers...there were still maybe five or six. The orcs had hardly taken any losses.

But how had it come to this in the first place...?

When they'd first descended to the first floor and then climbed the stairs to the watchtowers, Zoran had been nowhere to be seen. Had he been hiding somewhere?

There were doors on the first floor leading to places other than the stairs. All of those doors were open. That meant that volunteer soldiers had at least checked them for orcs. But they'd never found Zoran.

Maybe there was a secret basement or something. Zoran and his men could have hidden there, then come out when the volunteer soldiers went up to the towers. That could be it.

Zoran's attendants, including the three sorcerers, were around twenty people in total. Their strength was clearly a full level or two above the other orcs the volunteer soldiers had encountered today. They were a group of elites.

Team Renji was five people, and there were six—no, five other volunteer soldiers. Then there were Haruhiro and his party, for another six. The enemies outnumbered them, and they were probably stronger on average, too.

But is this... Is the difference in strength a hopeless one? Haruhiro wondered.

It wouldn't be long before the remaining volunteer soldiers were struck down, and then Renji and his party would fall one after another, rendering the situation hopeless. But now? Right now? At this point in time?

...At this point in time... he thought.

Assets. Not all of our strategic assets are here now. Kajiko and her Wild Angels probably haven't come down from the watchtower yet. Their force had a total of eighteen people. Even if they've lost a few, that's still around fifteen. Kajiko seemed tough, so maybe it'll be possible to turn things around when they come.

What about Bri-chan? He said something about checking on the main force. The detached force was originally supposed to serve as a diversion and to keep the enemy in check, with the main force breaking down the main gate and then taking the fortress. They've been delayed due to some unknown issue, but the main force ought to be here eventually. When they arrive, we're guaranteed to have the upper hand.

Do we wait until then? If we hide out in a watchtower until the main force arrives—No. We don't know when they might arrive, and if all of Team Renji goes down before then, that'd be bad. If that happens, the enemy is sure to search the keep for any remaining humans. Even if we're up in a watchtower, they'll find us eventually.

We can't rely on the main force.

But I want to count on Kajiko.

Then should we stay here until Kajiko comes down? It's a question of whether Renji and the others can hold out until then. To be honest, I want them to hang in there somehow. I don't want to take any more risks.

We stay here. Renji holds out. Kajiko comes. The tables are turned. That would be ideal, but there's no guarantee it will happen.

I want to save Team Renji, too, of course. Our party might be inconsequential small fry next to Renji, but we arrived in the same group. Renji and his party are being pushed to the brink. If I know that—no, more than know, I'm watching that—and then I do nothing, I'll have trouble sleeping at night afterward.

Besides, as assets in combat, we need Renji and his party to stick around.

I don't know how good Kajiko and her Wild Angels are, but if Team Renji and the other volunteer soldiers get wiped out, they'll have equal numbers, or even be at a slight disadvantage. Zoran's crazy strong, so I can't imagine Kajiko's guaranteed to win a fight like that. If Kajiko and the Wild Angels lose, our lives will be at risk.

How long have I been thinking for? I don't know. But there's no time to dawdle around. That much is for sure. I'd better hurry. We'll decide what we're going to do.

If he did nothing, Haruhiro—no, he and everyone else in his party—would die. That meant they were practically half-dead already. When he thought of it that way, it made things easier somehow.

Choco. I may be seeing you soon. When that happens, let's have a good long talk and recall the things we've forgotten one at a time.

Haruhiro went back to his comrades.

"Sorry, guys," he said. "I know it's scary, but let's keep trying a little longer. We're going to help Renji and the others. We'll focus solely on the sorcerers. Aside from their sorcery, they're nothing special."

He left out the "I think." He deliberately chose to assert it as fact. He felt like that was being deceptive to his comrades, but also to himself. But for some reason, he didn't have a guilty conscience over it.

"One of those sorcerers is probably that Abael guy," he continued. "He's worth fifty gold coins. We can't get Zoran, but we can kill Abael. Let's take it. Our fifty gold."

"Fiiiiifty! Gold! Yeahhhhhhhh!" Ranta shouted.

It was a good thing Ranta was so simple. With gold coins spinning in his eyes, he rushed down the stairs.

Haruhiro slapped Moguzo on the back. "Come on, Moguzo. We're counting on you."

"Mmhm!" He gave a manly response, which surprised Haruhiro a bit. Moguzo then followed after Ranta.

Haruhiro nodded to Merry, Yume, and Shihoru.

Is this all right? he wondered. *It is.*

When they finished descending the spiral staircase and set foot on the first floor, they immediately spotted a sorcerer.

They'd take them out one by one.

Haruhiro pointed at Sorcerer A. "That guy!"

Zoran and his orc attendants didn't even pay attention to them. Haruhiro and the party charged forward as a group. Sorcerer A noticed Haruhiro and the others. He tried to open his pot, but it was too late.

"Anger!" Ranta skewered Sorcerer A's throat with his longsword.

We're off to an auspicious start, Haruhiro thought. *But we can't let it go to our heads. We have to keep our heads level, and stick to killing them one by one.*

One of the orc attendants came at them, but Moguzo let out a battle cry and blew him away.

A sorcerer, Haruhiro thought. *Found one.*

"Him next!" he shouted, pointing at Sorcerer B.

As soon as he did, the orc attendants started to converge on them.

They're onto us, Haruhiro thought. *Well, even if they are, we have to finish the job.*

They didn't engage with the orc attendants. Moguzo howled and charged forward, cutting open a path, while Haruhiro used Swat to let him dash past them.

"Ohm, rel, ect, nemun, darsh!" Shihoru shouted. She used Shadow Bond to stop an orc attendant, while Merry cried out and smashed another orc attendant's shield with her priest's staff to force it aside.

"Star Piercer, meow!" Yume shouted as a series of throwing knives made the orc attendants back off and—

Wait, meow? What are you meowing for? Haruhiro thought. *Oh, whatever.*

Ranta was the first one to get close to Sorcerer B. This was where that technique showed up.

"Exhaust Plus!" Ranta did an about face in front of Sorcerer B, then leapt backwards.

From Sorcerer B's perspective, the human who'd come to attack him suddenly turned tail, then the next thing he knew, there was a butt flying at him. It must've been quite the shock.

Sorcerer B was hit full on by Ranta's hip attack and nearly fell over.

Now, Haruhiro thought.

He dashed past Sorcerer B's side.

Here. When he buried the dagger he was holding backhandedly into the nape of Sorcerer B's neck, he felt it connect with something. He'd stolen Sassa's best move, a Backstab as she passed by the enemy.

Sorcerer B crumpled.

"We've taken out two sorcerers!" Haruhiro bellowed.

Hearing that, Team Renji and the surviving volunteer soldiers seemed to come back to life, pushing back against the enemy.

It's the flow, Haruhiro thought. *The flow's on our side.*

Don't let your guard down, don't get carried away, Haruhiro kept telling himself. Still, he also felt that if he let this chance slip by, he'd regret it. Which was the right answer? He didn't know. But the situation would continue to change while he agonized about it. He didn't have time to worry about making the wrong choice.

"We can win!" he shouted.

We're going to ride this flow.

"We can win!" he shouted again. "Push through!"

Look, he thought. *Once the flow is on our side, things like this happen.*

"Eryeeeeeeeeeeeeeeeeeeeeeeeeeeeeeeeeeeee...!" a voice screamed.

There it is, he thought. *That scary voice. Kajiko. It's Kajiko and her group.*

The Wild Angels came down from the watchtower with Kajiko at the lead. In their first charge, they didn't so much cut down two of the orc attendants as demolished them. That was the kind of impression they left.

They could do this.

This was going to work out. This was the pattern for a total victory. That was what he thought, but...

As the Wild Angels swarmed onto the first floor, the third and final sorcerer, who must have been Abael, let loose that flamethrower again.

That wasn't all. Abael also threw something.

A rope? Haruhiro thought. *No. It's moving. Snakes. Those are snakes. More than just one or two of them.*

The sorcerer threw a large number of snakes at the Wild Angels' feet. There were screams. The Wild Angels were panicking.

Then Zoran Zesh abandoned Renji and charged in, slashing, slashing, and slashing like crazy. It was over in an instant. Four, then five of the lady warriors were mowed down.

"Don't falter!" Kajiko shouted, trying to stop Zoran.

They traded blows. Kajiko's sword intertwined with Zoran's twin blades. Sparks flew.

She backed down. Kajiko did. But it wasn't so much that she'd backed down herself, as that she'd been forced back.

"Damn!" she screamed. "We can't take any more losses! Everyone except Mako, Kikuno, and Azusa, withdraw for now!"

It seemed Kajiko intended to have the rest withdraw, keeping only the most experienced with her. Renji chased after Zoran, trying to get a slash in, but it was easily deflected.

Zoran's treating him like a child, Haruhiro realized. *Treating Renji like a child. Nah, Renji is injured. He's short of breath, too. He must be exhausted. Someone should do something about his wounds. It looks like Chibi-chan is treating Ron with her light magic. Light magic. The Heal spell can cure wounds from a distance. A priest. We have one. A priest other than Chibi-chan.*

"Merry! Use your magic on Renji!" he shouted.

"Heal won't work if he's moving! It targets an area!" she yelled back.

"It targets an area..." he murmured.

I see. Heal is a spell that makes healing light shine on a specific place. Until the light heals your wounds, you need to stay put there. Renji's fighting Zoran. There's no way he can stay still in one place.

"Still, we've got to let Renji rest a little!" Haruhiro called.

"Me! I'm your man!" a voice shouted.

That wasn't Ranta. It was Moguzo.

He seemed to be stressing his manliness. *I'm your man,* he'd said.

Moguzo roared and howled as he charged fiercely into Zoran.

Those hits are incredible, Haruhiro thought. *They're fast. Each and every blow is heavy. He's like Death Spots. Zoran's on the defensive now.*

Renji immediately tried to attack Zoran.

Come on! What do you think Moguzo's fighting so hard for?! Haruhiro thought, grabbing Renji by the arm.

"No! Come get healed!" he shouted.

"...Out of the way," Renji snapped.

"I'm not moving! Merry!"

"Right!" Merry rushed over while making the sign of the hexagram, then held her palm up towards Renji. "—O Light, may Lumiaris' divine protection be upon you... Cure!"

Bathed in the light of Lumiaris, Renji seemed to have resigned himself to it and didn't move. Merry directed her palm to the wounds on Renji's head, shoulders, and sides, healing them as she went. She healed and healed, but there was no sign of it ending. His breathing was ragged, and he was looking pale. Renji had bled out too much.

Ranta was fighting an orc attendant. Yume was with a different orc attendant. Yet another orc attendant started attacking Shihoru. Haruhiro hurriedly intervened, using Swat to buy time.

"Enough!" Renji struck down the orc that was attacking Haruhiro with one swing of Ish Dogran's sword, then took off running towards Zoran. "I'll take over, you dull-witted oaf! That's my prey!"

"No! Don't try to handle things all by yourself!" Moguzo cried.

Moguzo quickly shifted to the left of Zoran, leaving an opening on the right. Renji filled in that gap as if being sucked in and it turned into a two on one fight.

"I'm *not* a dull-witted oaf!" Moguzo added.

Moguzo attacked, swinging The Chopper around left and right. He continued his assault without ever giving his enemy a moment to catch his breath.

Renji made the sword of Ish Dogran dance, too. Moguzo was sturdy while Renji was flexible. Moguzo had power while Renji had skill. That was how it looked. It was all Zoran could do to use his twin blades to fend off both of their swords. It seemed like it couldn't possibly be true.

But it was. This was real.

"Yeah! That's right!" Haruhiro shouted. "You're no dull-witted oaf! You're doing great, Moguzo!"

He was like a totally different person. No. Maybe *this* was Moguzo. Moguzo had probably often been called slow, or dull-witted, and a lot of other nasty things. It had probably happened before he'd come to Grimgar, so he may not have remembered it, but he'd internalized those insults, and Moguzo had lost confidence in himself. But by fighting alongside Haruhiro and the others, he had become a great— almost *too* great—central pillar of the party.

Without Haruhiro there, the party could function so long as Merry or someone else took over as leader, but without Moguzo, they'd be in trouble. None of them could replace him. Everyone felt that way; they all relied on Moguzo.

Moguzo must've sensed the trust his comrades had for him, and now, he was fully aware of it. He was building confidence, and was finally able to show off his abilities.

This must be Moguzo's natural level of ability. Renji had misjudged him. Moguzo should've been brought onto Team Renji.

However, Renji's loss was their gain, as that meant Haruhiro and the others were able to have him in their party. In fact, perhaps Haruhiro ought to be grateful for the good fortune that'd brought Moguzo and the rest of them together.

"I don't like fighting alongside men, but...!" Kajiko butted in, attacking Zoran from behind.

Zoran leapt to the side and ran.

That Zoran was running away.

"The bounty's an even split!" she called.

"Get lost!" Renji shouted.

"Rarrrrrgh...!" Moguzo added.

Kajiko, Renji, and Moguzo all chased after Zoran.

They could do this. This might work out.

The moment Haruhiro thought that, Ranta caught on fire, tumbled to the ground, and flipped over. "Whoa! Gwahhhhhhhhhhhhhhhhhh...!"

It was the sorcerer. Sorcerer Abael.

Abael had caught Ranta with his flamethrower, then immediately turned and run off.

That guy's fast, Haruhiro thought. *What's more, he faithfully follows a hit-and-run strategy. Thanks to that, he's hard to catch.*

"Merry, go to Ranta!" he shouted.

"I know!" she called.

"Yume, defend Shihoru!" he added.

"Meow!"

"What's 'meow' supposed to mean?!" He didn't really get it, but she was staying next to Shihoru, so it must've meant "yes."

"Ohm, rel, ect, palam, darsh!" Shihoru used Shadow Complex to confuse one of the orc attendants, but it wasn't enough to make a difference. The orcs still had more than ten of the attendants, plus Zoran and Abael, while they had the five members of Team Renji, the six members of Haruhiro's party, the four members from Kajiko's Wild Angels, and three other volunteer soldiers—

Huh? We're winning? If you only look at the numbers, we're winning, aren't we? Haruhiro thought.

But then Abael caught another volunteer soldier with his flamethrower.

"Arrrrgh...!" The volunteer soldier screamed, bursting into flames and then falling to the ground.

Someone'd better heal him, or he's in danger, Haruhiro thought. *Wait, that volunteer soldier is wearing the priest uniform. It's burning, though. If he's a priest, can he heal himself? Probably not when he's like that. But neither Chibi-chan or Merry can afford to go heal him.*

"It's Abael!" Haruhiro called. "We've gotta finish that guy!"

Moguzo, Renji, and Kajiko were preoccupied with Zoran. Ron couldn't leave Sassa, Chibi-chan, and Adachi.

"Mako-san, Kikuno-san, Azusa-san!" Haruhiro shouted. "Go after the sorcerer first!"

He happened to remember their names, so Haruhiro tried calling out to the women from the Wild Angels. They were each facing an orc attendant on their own. One of them, a woman as big as Kajiko who looked like a warrior, was heartily beating down an orc attendant.

Perhaps that was the moment Abael had been waiting for. He swiftly moved up closer to her, opening the lid on the pot he carried.

Bugs, Haruhiro remembered. But before Haruhiro could warn her, the bugs ambushed the large woman.

"Eeeeek!" the woman screamed, trying to brush the bugs off

herself.

It was reflexive, no doubt, so it was hard to blame her, but this was bad. She needed to run or something and fast. This time, Abael didn't withdraw immediately. He was closing in on her, trying to do something.

Hey, wait, couldn't this be an opportunity...? The moment that thought occurred to him, Haruhiro was running.

Abael was carrying a short, metal mace. He used it to strike the woman in the knees, then followed it up with a hard blow to the head. The woman was wearing a helmet, so it wasn't clear if it was a fatal blow or not, but she slumped to the ground.

Abael turned around, looking in Haruhiro's direction.

Damn, Haruhiro thought. *He noticed me.*

"Gashgrasha!" Abael shouted and swung his mace.

It's short, I can dodge it, Haruhiro thought, but his body reacted in an exaggerated manner. He threw himself to the floor, rolling over and then getting up, but by that time Abael was already fleeing.

"He's fast!" Haruhiro cried.

After that, he started to give chase.

Is this really all right? Haruhiro wondered. *I don't know whether it's good or bad. But if I let him act freely, he'll only do more damage. We'll be taken down one by one, and our numerical advantage will eventually vanish.*

It's scary, though.

Could someone like Haruhiro stop an enemy like that?

I certainly don't think I can handle him on my own. I mean, look at that.

Abael turned towards him, and Haruhiro dove to the floor once again.

It's coming, he thought, and he was right. It was flames. A flamethrower. Had he reacted even a moment slower, Haruhiro would have been burned to a crisp.

Abael ran away again. Haruhiro quickly resumed his pursuit, but the gap had widened between them.

Y'know...this may be hopeless, he thought. *It's not looking like I can do it.*

I can't catch him, and even if I did, what am I even going to do? I'm worried about my comrades, too, but if I take my eyes off Abael for a second, I feel like I'll lose sight of him.

As Abael ran, he seemed to be peeking back occasionally to check on Haruhiro.

I'll lose sight of him. Haruhiro stopped.

"Osh!" An orc attendant took a swing at him.

Haruhiro dodged the orc attendant's blade, turning around and taking the calculated risk of running straight towards another of the orc attendants. He made a sudden turn just before he entered his new opponent's reach, and the two attendants almost ran into one another.

While that was happening, Haruhiro got away from them. He looked around, making sure not to stop moving as he did.

Lose sight of him? he thought. *Not a chance. The first floor's big, but it's only so big. If I look for him, I can find him in no time.*

Despite that, Abael would vanish. He'd disappear, then suddenly reappear. Of course, he couldn't actually vanish. He left their field of view, then mixed in with the other orcs, making it look like he'd disappeared. Then, once they forgot about him, he'd launch a surprise attack.

Haruhiro had given up on Abael. That was what he needed Abael to think. For Abael, Haruhiro would disappear. If he did that, Abael would go on the attack again.

Haruhiro wasn't looking at Abael anymore—or so he pretended.

Looks like Abael plans to go towards Ron and his group, he thought. *Either that, or the two Wild Angels who were now alone together. Or possibly Moguzo, or Renji, or Kajiko. It's difficult to tell from the way he moves.*

Is that how he gets up close to his targets? I'll imitate him. No—I'm a thief. I'll steal that from him.

A moment later, he'd figured it out. *That's who Abael's next target is*—*the one who's being protected by Ron and Chibi-chan while he uses Kanon magic to disrupt the orc attendants and give them frostbite. It's Adachi.*

Abael locked his sights on Adachi, preparing to catch him with a blast of flame, but Haruhiro went for a Backstab right before he could.

Abael gasped and twisted out of the way at the last moment. Haruhiro's dagger only managed to gouge Abael's left arm.

Haruhiro had screwed it up, but Abael didn't fight back. He ran away immediately.

Does he only fight when he's at an absolute advantage? Haruhiro thought. *He's committed to that. I don't know whether to call that cowardly or clever. He's cunning.*

Abael had probably seen through Haruhiro's plan. Haruhiro had stolen Abael's methods and copied them, but the cat had to be out of the bag now. The same trick wouldn't work again. If he let him get away now, Abael would grow more cautious and there might not be another opening to take him out.

"Exhaust Plus!" Ranta screamed.

"Ubogeh?!" Abael exclaimed.

For a moment, Abael must not have known what hit him. Most people wouldn't expect a human butt flying toward the side of their head at extreme speeds.

The solid hit from Ranta's hip attack sent Abael pitching forward.

Still, how does Ranta have such ridiculously good timing sometimes? Haruhiro wondered. *It's too good. You're creeping me out, man. Anyway, I don't need to be able to see that line to be able to kill Abael now.*

Haruhiro took every possible caution, choosing to use Spider instead of Backstab. He grappled Abael from behind, putting him in a pinion. He then shoved his dagger under the orc's chin, violently slitting the orc's throat open before immediately leaping away.

"Smirk!" Ranta said aloud.

Is he an idiot? Haruhiro thought. *Well, yes, I know he is, but still.*

Ranta swung his longsword down diagonally, slamming it into the back of Abael's neck. It may not have decapitated the orc, but it went about halfway through.

He kicked the orc to the ground, then followed up with another strike. Not satisfied with one, he went for a second, then a third. Abael stopped moving.

"Yes! fifty gold!" Ranta screamed. "Oh, also, a vice, too!"

That's Ranta for you, Haruhiro thought. *He never breaks character. You almost have to admire the guy. Well, I won't. There's no way I would.*

"Now it's just Zoran!" Haruhiro called.

There are still orc attendants left, but Zoran Zesh comes first. With the danger Abael posed gone now, and them fighting Zoran three on one, we can do this.

"Moguz—Whoa...?!" Haruhiro exclaimed.

Just as he'd been starting to cheer, Zoran leapt. It was a forward somersault.

Kajiko tried to take a swing at his back but missed, while Renji and Moguzo who were in front of him leapt backwards.

"Wha—?!" Kajiko yelled.

"Urkh!" Renji yelped.

"Oh...?!" Moguzo gasped.

"Gahhhhhhhhhhhhhhhhhhhhhhhhhhhhhhhhhhh...!"   Zoran roared.

Then the orc spun. His forward somersault had used a vertical spin, but now he was moving forward while whirling around like a top. His spin was horizontal this time.

It was fast. With incredible momentum. It wasn't that Renji and Moguzo didn't do anything. They backed away. But they couldn't get back far enough. They both tried to block Zoran's twin blades with their swords and were sent flying.

Zoran wasted no time in attacking Moguzo. It was a relentless onslaught. When Renji tried to step in and help, Zoran immediately turned towards him and attacked. After forcing him to back off with a powerful slash, he wailed on Moguzo with his twin blades.

"Eryeeeeeeeeeeeeeeeeeeeeeeeeeeeeeeeeeeee!"   Kajiko   attacked Zoran from behind. But Zoran took a swing or two at her as he turned around, bouncing her back, then attacked Moguzo again.

Moguzo. Moguzo. Zoran persistently focused his attack entirely on Moguzo. When Renji tried to get between them, he used his forward somersault and spinning slash combo to make him back off, then returned to Moguzo.

Why? Haruhiro wondered numbly. *Why is he so focused on him? Moguzo can barely block anymore. His armor is all dented. His helmet is crushed. He's being ground down. Moguzo is. Second by second. Of course I want to do something. But what can I do?*

Perhaps emboldened by Zoran's attack, his attendants pushed in closer, chanting, "Osh, osh!" One of the attendants attacked Haruhiro. He was defending himself with Swat, but this guy was strong. Haruhiro felt like his dagger was going to be sent flying.

"Parupiro!" Ranta shouted.

Ranta came to his aid right in the nick of time, which got Haruhiro out of a jam, but Ranta's calling him "Parupiro" was not okay. Ranta had saved him, though.

"Gah!" Kajiko screamed. Zoran got in a hit with his sword, and Kajiko's helmet came off. Her face was covered in fresh blood.

"Get back!" Renji yelled at her.

I dunno if that's Mako, or Kikuno, or Azusa, but she's dragging Kajiko away, Haruhiro thought. *This is no good. It's no good at all. I was sure we had it this time.*

He's too damn strong. Zoran Zesh. Ish Dogran was like nothing next to him. He's a monster.

But somehow—I dunno. There's something strange, you could say, or something that bothers me. His balance.

Yeah. It's his balance. The balance of what? His body. Left and right. The balance between his left and right. Left—he spins left. When he turns around, Zoran always turns to the left. And yet, when he does his spinning slash, it's the opposite. He spins right. Why? It's weird. Something about it bugs me.

"Paroporo!" Ranta screamed. "Quit standing there like an idiot!"

This is no time to stand around like an idiot, Haruhiro thought. *Well, yeah, he's right. I'm not Paroporo, though.*

Ranta was right in what he was saying, but Haruhiro kept thinking.

This is important. I get that feeling.

Those twin blades. Is Zoran left-handed? Left-handed? Why did I think that?

It's because they're stiff. His movements. When he moves his left arm, it seems more fluid than his right. His right arm moves up and down less, like it's stiff. Either that, or like it's under some weird stress.

Like he's trying to cover something.

If, for example, he has an old wound on his right shoulder or right side, could that be what's causing it? Even if it was unconsciously, he'd naturally try to cover it.

Well, so what?

Renji and Moguzo, who were desperately confronting him from up close, probably wouldn't notice it. Haruhiro had only noticed it by chance because he was watching from a distance.

Again, so what? he thought.

"Ranta!" Haruhiro called.

"Huh?!" Ranta asked.

"Do you want a hundred gold?!"

"Damn straight I do!" Ranta yelled.

"Then be a decoy!" Haruhiro told him. "You're the only one who can do it!"

"Ha! Looks like you've finally figured out how to use me properly!" Ranta hollered. "What do you need done?!"

Haruhiro gave him a brief explanation. Ranta's role was dangerous, but simple. With a dread knight doing it, even if it didn't work, just attempting it wouldn't be that difficult. The problem was Moguzo and Renji.

"Moguzo! Renji!" Haruhiro shouted. "He has a habit of turning to the left when he turns around, and his right side is weak! He's got an old wound there or something! Let Ranta take the front! You two get behind him!"

Would they get it? Even if they understood, could they do it? There was no guarantee.

Haruhiro looked over towards Merry and the others. Merry and Yume were working together to stop an orc attendant and protect Shihoru. Shihoru used Shadow Bond to stop another orc attendant in his tracks. It was good just knowing they were alive.

...Choco, Haruhiro thought. *Choco's fallen. She's dead.*

Once you die, that's the end.

Let's end this.

I'm going to settle things.

"We're doing this, Ranta!" he shouted. "Are you ready?!"

"Hell yeah!" Ranta hollered. "It's 150 gold!"

"*That's* your response?!"

Haruhiro ran. Zoran followed Haruhiro with his eyes while continuing to rain harsh blows on Moguzo and Renji. He was perceptive. Haruhiro was trying to circle around behind Zoran.

He's seen through me, Haruhiro thought. *But how about this?*

"Hey, loser!" Ranta came out in front of Zoran. "I can handle you all by myself, you damn loser! Did you hear me, loser? Loooo-ser, loooo-ser, loooo-seeeer!"

He stood in front of Zoran, pointing his sword at him and striking a grand pose. It was all according to their script, but still, so crass.

Still, with Ranta taking it that far, Zoran had to know he was being insulted, even if he couldn't understand the words. Maybe that was what made him snap. Zoran used a forward somersault, followed by a spinning slash.

"Gahhhhhhhhhhhhhhhhhhhhhhhhhhhhhhhhhhhhhhh...!" Zoran roared.

"Exhaust!" Ranta wasn't blown away. He blasted himself backwards, evading Zoran's spinning slash, or flying out of range of it. "Ha! Moron, you're so obvious, you loooo—whoa, Exhaust...!"

Ranta had gotten carried away and Zoran had chased after him in a rage. It'd only take Zoran an instant to cover the distance that Ranta could fall back using Exhaust.

Still, Haruhiro had been right. Moguzo and Renji were both more powerful in combat than Ranta, of course. In a one-on-one fight, Ranta would absolutely lose. Even so, those two weren't superior to Ranta at everything. Ranta had things he was better at than they were.

When Zoran launched his forward-somersault-and-spinning-slash combo, Moguzo and Renji couldn't avoid it. They were forced to block with their swords. It hadn't just happened the first time. It'd happened repeatedly.

Moguzo and Renji were by no means slow. Even if they knew it was coming, they couldn't get out of the way. Zoran's combo was just that fast, and its reach was long, which made it dangerous. Despite that, Ranta had shown he could dodge it.

The way his Exhaust skill worked played into that, but, at the very least, when it came to dodging that combo, Ranta the dread knight was superior to Renji and Moguzo the warriors.

"Gahhhhhhhhhhhh! Gahhhhhhhhhhhhhhhh...!" the orc roared.

"Exhaust! Exhaust!" Ranta bellowed.

Zoran was getting mad. He couldn't even hit someone like Ranta, so it was easy to see why that'd make him angry.

Thanks to that, Haruhiro was able to get behind Zoran. Moguzo and Renji were both chasing Zoran along with Haruhiro.

"He spins to the left, remember!" Haruhiro called.

If they were going to attack, he thought, it should be from the right. Compared to attacking from the left or from right behind him, Zoran's sword would take just slightly longer to reach them.

"Wah ha ha!" Ranta hollered. "You're not good enough to beat me!"

As Ranta incorrigibly continued his provocations, Zoran howled and executed a combo. A forward somersault, then a spinning slash.

Ranta escaped with Exhaust yet again.

Just as the spinning slash was ending, Renji came at Zoran from his right side. His attack was quiet, swift, sharp, and fierce. He seemed to creep in, yet he closed the distance rapidly, then swung his blade.

Zoran reacted with a spin to the left, of course. Using the sword in his left hand, his back hand, you could say, he swung to the outside to deflect Renji's sword. It was so close.

Making it by a hair's breadth, Zoran's sword blocked Renji's.

But it was different from before. While Renji's blade may not have reached Zoran's body, it pushed Zoran's sword aside.

Though, that said, Zoran was a dual-wielder. Zoran quickly swept Renji's torso with his right-hand sword. Renji had probably put everything he had into that one strike. He'd abandoned his defense.

He couldn't dodge.

"Guh...!" Renji gasped.

It must have been thanks to his armor. He didn't get cut in two. Still, it was a direct hit. Renji was mowed down.

It's a failure, Haruhiro thought. *It didn't work.*

Haruhiro slowed down and was about to stop running. Moguzo, however, didn't.

"Thanks...!"

But Moguzo was being reckless. It was his Thanks Slash, or Rage Blow. He dug his feet in, swinging down diagonally and slashing with all his might.

It wasn't a surprise attack. Zoran was ready for it. He waited for the opportune moment, not even bothering to use his swords to catch the blow. Zoran's blade was faster than Moguzo's.

He first struck Moguzo's right shoulder. Then his upper right arm, left forearm, and right hip. Then, he went for the head. The left side, then the top of it.

Plated armor and helmets are that sturdy, huh? Haruhiro thought with relief. *He can't cut through them. But even if he can't cut through, there's no way Moguzo's fine after that. There are huge dents all over his armor.*

Still, even though there's no way he's fine, Moguzo's not going down. He won't even take a knee. He's standing there like he's dug his feet in hard. Oh, I see.

Steel Guard.

The heavy armor skill that uses armor and defensive items to their fullest, and then some, by bouncing back enemy attacks.

However, no matter how I look at it, those attacks aren't being bounced back. He's taking a one-sided clobbering. Can he withstand that? No matter how tough Moguzo is, he can't take that for long. In that case...

There was only one thing for Haruhiro to do.

His body was already moving on its own.

Haruhiro was a thief. He was a coward who was always watching his opponents' backs, always thinking about how to get behind them, and now was no different.

Zoran was focusing on Moguzo. He must've been wondering why this human just wouldn't go down. It was strange. Wrong. Just maybe, he was feeling a creepiness from it. He may even have been being driven by irritation and impatience.

Haruhiro charged in towards Zoran's back.

The line? I can't see that thing, he thought. *It doesn't matter. However, I do have a vague sense of where to strike. Zoran's wearing some high-quality red armor and a helmet, but there's a slight gap between the two. Maybe I can get in through here?*

Zoran was tall, so Haruhiro held his dagger with a backhanded grip, then swung down. He aimed for the seam between his head and back.

He stabbed.

In that moment, Zoran's body stiffened.

Haruhiro pulled his dagger free, getting ready to stab again, when Zoran's left arm came at him and he was knocked away.

"Thanks...!" Moguzo bellowed.

As Haruhiro was rolling across the floor, Moguzo unleashed his Thanks Slash and landed a hit on the tip of Zoran's shoulder. Zoran kicked Moguzo away and might've been trying to make a temporary retreat.

I won't let you. Haruhiro clung to Zoran's right leg.

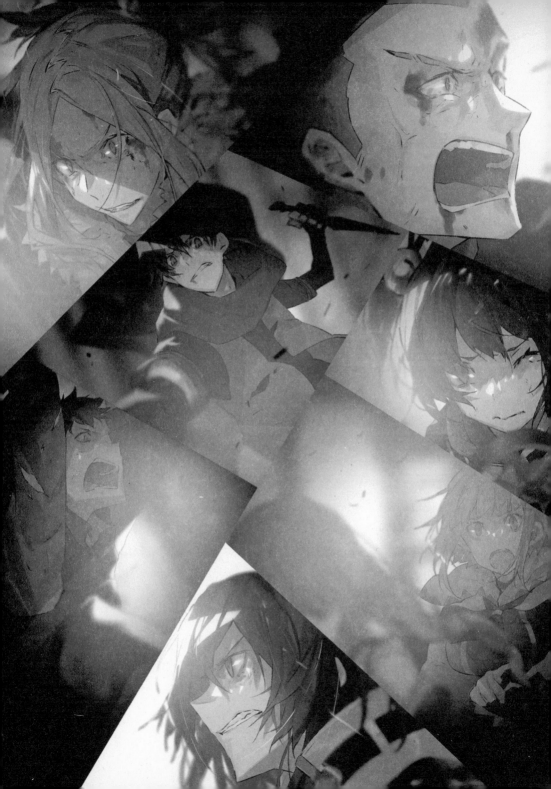

Zoran immediately stomped on Haruhiro's head with the heel of his right foot, knocking him senseless for a moment.

When he came to, Kajiko was showering blows on Zoran. Ron was nearby, too. Adachi unleashed Kanon magic on Zoran. Chibi-chan bludgeoned Zoran with her staff.

Ranta slashed him. Shihoru used Shadow Beat. Yume hit Zoran with her machete. Even Merry was there using her priest's staff to clobber Zoran.

Because of the blow to his head, Haruhiro was feeling a little out of it.

Huh, that's a little weird, he thought. *Everyone is wailing on Zoran as if they were possessed. Well, I can't blame them. We've had a terrifying experience. A lot of people have died. Seriously, that guy is so terrifying, it's not even funny. Now Zoran's cowering on the ground, not resisting.*

Is he still alive? I wonder. What about his attendants? It looks like some of them tried to save Zoran, but they got taken out. You know, there aren't a lot of attendants. No, that's not it—there are a lot more of us.

The rest of the Wild Angels and some volunteer soldiers who had been hiding came out. They surrounded Zoran's attendants one by one and beat them to death.

Haruhiro touched the back of his head. He wasn't bleeding. But his face was all wet. It looked like his head, nose, or jaw had hit the floor when Zoran had stomped his head, and he was bleeding from that. It was hard to breathe, so maybe his nose was broken.

"Enough!" Renji stood up, pushing his way past Kajiko, the members of Team Renji, and Haruhiro's party.

Ranta yelled something and tried to stop him, but Renji just punched him.

Renji grabbed the Sword of Ish Dogran. No one had time to stop him. He swung down, decapitating Zoran.

"It's over," he said.

The room was silent.

"Wooooo!" someone cheered.

The few remaining attendants shouted something before charging the Wild Angels, only to be slaughtered.

"Haru!" Merry rushed over to him. "Are you okay?!"

Haruhiro nodded. He tried to say something, but he couldn't speak.

"150!" Ranta cried, jumping into the air in joy. "150 gold!"

"Renji struck the killing blow!" Sassa tried to protest, but Kajiko shouted, "It's an even split!"

I don't really think I care, Haruhiro thought. *Well, no, I do care. I mean, it's a fortune. We could learn new skills, or we could move out of the lodging house and rent at a place with doors that lock, or we could order new equipment; there are a lot of things we could do with it. Our defensive gear in particular is getting pretty battered. We need to get it fixed or replaced.*

Oh, but I'm not thinking straight.

It looked like the orc attendants had all been killed. Shihoru was crying tears of relief and Yume was hugging her, saying, "There, there. You did great. Just great," as she patted her on the head.

"Can you get up?" Merry asked him.

Yeah, no, I can't. Haruhiro was about to say that lie, because it seemed like Merry would treat him gently that way. But he didn't.

"I can manage, yeah," Haruhiro said, getting up. "Though, really, before you help me..."

Why's he just standing there? Haruhiro wondered.

Everyone was dancing, chatting, having their priest treat them, or doing something, but Moguzo was just standing there.

There's something weird about it, Haruhiro thought.

Moguzo wasn't holding his sword. His arms were slumped at his sides.

It's incredible that he's standing at all, though, Haruhiro thought. *I'm amazed he can stand. That he managed to stay on his feet. Especially in that state. Like, his helmet, it's not just crushed, it's not even on completely. There's blood dripping off him here and there, too.*

Suddenly, Moguzo slowly fell over. Like when something big and heavy suddenly loses its support and collapses. That was the sort of fall it was.

Merry gulped.

Haruhiro called his name. "...Moguzo?"

afterword

I am, thankfully, able to make a living writing novels.

For some reason, I've received a steady stream of offers from different people, which has put me in the privileged environment of being able to support my lifestyle just by writing the manuscripts that I need to work on. It keeps me fairly busy, but if I set my mind to it, I can make as much time for myself as I'd like, so the reason I constantly keep writing is because I enjoy it.

When I find myself without work to do for a day or two, rather than play through all the games I've bought and set aside, I think of how to make the ideas I've been incubating into novels.

There's basically no distinction between work and play for me. I've never had many friends to begin with, so for me play meant playing video games by myself, so writing novels by myself is a kind of play, too.

Of course, the experience of writing novels isn't always fun. It can be painful, difficult work. However, even with video games, there are times where you just can't beat them and you struggle. The joy of overcoming those challenges and beating a game, that feeling of release, is incredible.

It's the same with novels. When you go through hardship to finish writing them, it's very rewarding.

I am half—no, more than half—making my living by playing around. I often run into difficult situations while writing, but I've overcome them many times before, and I take the relatively optimistic view that I'll continue to overcome them. Even if I make a mistake, it's not like I'm fighting on the battlefield, so it's not going to kill me, and I'm sure I'll have chances to redeem myself. Well, I'll get by somehow.

I no longer play games the way I once did. This is probably the reason why. For me games were, at least for a time, the only kind of play I knew. But now I play by writing novels. Thanks to that, I don't have time to play games.

That said, I'm sure there are kinds of excitement and new experiences that I can only find through games. That's why, to this day, I continue to look for information on games. I buy the ones that interest me, play them for a bit, and then get a little disappointed when they don't live up to expectations. Still, I can never stop looking forward to my next experience with them. I'm sure I won't stop until the day I die.

I've run out of pages.

To my editor, K, to Eiri Shirai-san, to the designers of KOMEWORKS among others, to everyone involved in production and sales of this book, and finally to all of you people now holding this book, I offer my heartfelt appreciation and all of my love. Now, I lay down my pen for today.

I hope we will meet again.

Ao Jyumonji